THE BEWITCHING HOUR

Toni Blake

Dear Reader,

This is one of three books published at the beginning of my career under the pen name Toni Blair. Unfortunately, when they first released in the late 90s, the length limitations of the publisher required these novels to be shortened by approximately one-third of their original length, altering my vision for the stories significantly. So I'm pleased to be able to present, for the first time anywhere, the full and extended versions of these books.

As I read over my original manuscripts and polished up the words a little, I realized that I could not write these same books now—I discovered in them a certain youthfulness and innocence that came from just that, my youth, and my more limited worldview at the time. I'm a very different person and writer than I was then, and it was both enlightening and invigorating to revisit these stories, getting reacquainted with my younger writing self and seeing parts of myself I'd long since forgotten. As part of preserving the context of that worldview, I've chosen to keep this book in its original setting, not updating for technology or other lifestyle changes.

It is with great joy that I present to you *The Bewitching Hour* (originally published under the title *October Moon*) as I intended it to be read. I hope you will enjoy it!

Toni Blake

Chapter One

─────◆─────

"WEAR THE NOSE."

"I'm not wearing the nose."

"Wear it," Rhonda prodded. "The costume is nothing without it."

"That's just it," Julie replied, surveying herself in the antique floor-length mirror in her bedroom. "I'm not exactly sure I want to draw attention to myself in this."

She wore a form-fitting black dress, narrow to the knees, then flaring out at the bottom. Around her neck she donned a chain of plastic spiders, accented with matching eight-legged earrings above. Topping the outfit was a pointy black hat that seemed to reach the ceiling.

"The witch is a classic symbol of Halloween," Rhonda said in a tone reminiscent of a nature documentary.

Julie rolled her eyes at the mirror.

"It's a great costume," Rhonda went on. Then she reached into the shopping bag at her feet and pulled out a small black broom, which she shoved into Julie's hand. "There," she said. "You look great. But you should wear the nose."

"I'm not wearing the nose." Covered with crags and crevices and a hook at its bridge, the fleshy rubber nose also sported a huge wart on its tip. Julie intended to stand firm. "And if this costume is so great," she added, "how come *you're* not wearing it?"

"Because I'm the sexy devil," Rhonda replied, quoting the packing label that had come with her slinky costume. It was little more than a piece of silky red lingerie held on with spaghetti-thin straps. She shook her behind to jiggle the pointy red tail that hung from it. "And because beggars can't be choosers. People who decide they want to go to Halloween parties at the last minute have to be content with what I can find in my closet."

Julie glared at her friend, thinking how appropriate that Rhonda had dressed as a devil. The glittering red horns emerging from her auburn mane provided the perfect accent to the wicked twinkle in her eyes.

"Excuse me," Julie said, "but I don't exactly think I *decided* to go to this party. I think you decided for me. In fact, I think you're forcing me into it."

"Only to save you from yet another pathetic night of crying into your caramel apples, Jules. You need to get out, meet guys, make friends, have fun, meet guys."

"You said that one twice."

"Sorry, I was trying to be sneaky and plant subliminal messages in your head."

Julie turned back to the mirror, trying to decide if she should pull her dark, shoulder-length hair back into a barrette or let it stay loose.

And without being asked, Rhonda supplied an answer. "It's much cuter if you let it frame your face."

Julie nodded silently and brushed through the hair with her fingers, pulling some of the layered locks toward her cheeks.

"Now look," Rhonda continued, "if you won't wear the nose and be scary, at least put on a better bra and look sexy."

"What?" Julie asked, losing interest in her hair.

"That dress isn't low-cut for nothin', Jules. And whatever you're wearing under it is smashing you as flat as a pancake. Is that a sports bra or something?"

Julie watched as Rhonda helped herself to Julie's lingerie drawer, rifling through it until she found what she was looking for. She snatched out a black, lacy push-up bra, leaving what was once a neatly stacked collection of underwear in a shambles of white, pink, and black silk. "Aha!" she said, holding it up. "This should do it."

"But that's the bra I bought to wear to the ballet with Patrick last Christmas under my good black dress."

"So?"

"Well, it's sort of…for special occasions," Julie explained. Even though the night had not turned out to be so special. Patrick had been the only rowdy drunken man sitting in the third row at the Nutcracker yelling for the ballerinas to 'take it off.'

Rhonda shook her head skeptically at Julie's claim of saving a bra for a special occasion. "Then pretend this *is* one," she instructed. "Your cleavage needs a boost, Jules."

"Thanks so much for noticing."

"It's not that there's anything wrong with them," Rhonda explained, "but you're not maximizing their potential. There are going to be a lot of nice single guys at this party."

"And you're suggesting that I should reel them in with my boobs?"

"It's a start. Men like them, you know."

"I prefer to be appreciated for my mind," Julie announced smugly.

"Well, that's great if you want to attract a guy with taped glasses and a pocket protector, but even *you* have better taste than that. Now, look, it's the bra or the nose, one or the other. Halloween rule: you dress as something funny, scary, or sexy. And you're definitely not either of the first two unless you wear the nose. I'm not letting up on this. Now what's it gonna be?"

Julie sighed. "You are infuriating," she said, plucking away the black bra that dangled from Rhonda's fingers.

Then she shoved her friend into the hallway, shutting the thick wooden door in her face. That was one advantage to living in an older home—a slamming door sounded solid and forceful, like it meant something. And at the moment, it was serving as a good way to take out her frustrations.

Alone, she unzipped the back of the too-snug witch dress and lowered it to her waist. Then she shed her boring stay-in-place white bra for the sexy black uplifting one. She turned back to the mirror.

It certainly did help the appearance of her breasts—that she couldn't deny. Swelling toward each other, they appeared much larger than their average size. Generally pert, the bra made them look downright firm, pretty, and sexy. She felt almost pleased until she pulled the dress back into place and zipped it up.

The bra helped provide more than enough cleavage to accent the curvy black costume. And Julie knew that if Rhonda had worn it, she'd have been a definite knockout. But Julie wasn't used to wearing something this sexy or revealing and she wasn't sure she could pull it off. She wasn't even certain that she wanted to. Could she actually leave the house looking this way?

She opened the door to let the she-devil back inside, and Rhonda's eyes gleamed with wicked delight as she gave her friend the once-over. "You look great, Jules. Really."

"I'm sure Patrick would love it," Julie mused dryly. He had pushed her to wear sexy, revealing things for the entire time they'd been together, but she'd seldom surrendered her casual, conservative style of dress, even for him. So it seemed terribly backward and ironic to start wearing such things now that he was gone.

"Well, this has nothing to do with Patrick," Rhonda reminded her. Which was true. *Nothing* she did had anything to do with Patrick anymore. He'd left her over four months ago. And she knew that she was better for it.

But the loss still hurt.

"I'm not sure I'm going to the party," she announced.

"What?" Rhonda snapped. "We're supposed to leave in half an hour."

"I don't wanna go," she whined. "This dress isn't me, these spiders aren't me, and this hat *certainly* isn't me. I'm not witchy, and I'm not sexy, and I don't want to do this."

Rhonda scrutinized her for a moment, then her voice grew stern. "Grow up," she said. "This isn't a junior high mixer. It's a grown-up party with grown-up people. So act grown-up about it."

"In *this*?" she asked, motioning with one hand down at the dress and with the other up at the too-tall hat.

"Look, I know you're afraid to re-enter the single world again, but you promised me you'd go and I counted on that. The only people I'll know at this bash are my old neighbors, so even as outgoing as you think I am, I can't walk into this place alone." Rhonda sighed and laced her fire-engine red fingernails together. "And besides," she added softly, "I'm only making you do this because I care about you and want to help you get over Patrick."

Julie tried to smirk, but couldn't. She hated it when Rhonda turned sincere. "I know," she finally conceded with a large sigh of her own.

"I mean, what you saw in Patrick, once you got beyond the initial charm, I'll never know. But it's over,

Jules, and you have to get on with your life."

Julie nodded, knowing full well that Rhonda was right, but still unable to verbalize her agreement. She'd been with the guy for over three years, after all. Even though he was a liar. And a cheat. And an all-around general jerk. Despite herself, she'd been in love with him. And even though she knew he was already living with and engaged to someone else—commitments he'd never been able to make to her—she still wasn't completely over him.

"Love stinks," Julie finally muttered.

"I know," Rhonda agreed. "It takes some time to get over a bad relationship. And some effort, too. Now, I'm telling you, wear the nose."

JULIE WALKED THROUGH her yard, leaves crunching beneath the heels of her shoes as an unseasonably warm autumn breeze swirled around her. *Nice weather for the trick-or-treaters tomorrow night.*

The quaint old neighborhood where she lived was a trick-or-treater's heaven. The streets were safe, the houses close together, and most of the families had lived there forever, long enough to know all the kids personally and to want to give them something special. That was why she'd started making candy apples each year.

She'd lived in the house for four years, a relative youngster to the neighborhood, and on her first Halloween there, she'd felt like a loser to discover she was the only homeowner on the street handing out packaged candy bars, and tiny ones at that. Some houses gave out brownies, others cookies, and Mrs. Jenkins next door handed out homemade pumpkin squares. Word was that Mr. Dover on the corner bought fifty silver dollars at the bank each year and that the first fifty kids to his door got them.

Since stumbling onto such bits of information, Julie had made caramel apples her trademark Halloween treat. Not terribly original, but she liked the traditional aspect and she was also pretty fond of caramel herself. It made the house smell delicious for days.

She looked to the darkened windows of her home as Rhonda backed the car from the driveway. It looked so warm in there. So safe.

So what if it was Saturday night? Who said you had to go out and do something fun just because of what night of the week it happened to be? She sighed, thinking how much she'd rather be back inside curled up by the fireplace in some cozy pajamas with a good book.

That had been one nice aspect of having Patrick out of her life. Lots of free time to do the things she liked to do, and the ability to truly be herself, not the person he'd tried so vehemently to mold her into. Which made her ask the question once more: *Why on earth am I going to this party?*

She was tempted to complain to Rhonda again, to again announce that she'd changed her mind and *wouldn't* be going, but would instead be immersing herself into the *New York Times* bestseller that rested on her coffee table. She stayed quiet, though, knowing the effort would be worthless. Rhonda and her sparkly devil horns were determined to do what they thought was best for her whether she liked it or not. And Rhonda had been right about one thing: you couldn't leave a friend high and dry when they were counting on you.

Still, she had misgivings and plenty of them. The whole idea of dressing up for parties at her age, as well as the fact that Rhonda felt it her duty to make sure Julie was doing something fun on Halloween, was appalling. *Thirty years old and my friends still think I'm incapable of handling my own life. Thirty years old and still going to parties looking for cute guys. How pathetic.*

"You think of me as an adult, don't you?" she asked as Rhonda maneuvered the leaf-strewn streets.

"Geez, I was only kidding when I told you to grow up," Rhonda said. "You're way more adult than me."

"You really think so?" Julie gazed out into the pathway the car's headlights carved through the darkness.

"God, yes. For one thing, you own your own business."

"True," Julie said. She'd bought the antique shop at twenty-three, a mere two years after earning a marketing degree only to discover that no one wanted her to market anything. Seven years later she was renowned as one of the top antique dealers in the state.

"And you have your own house," Rhonda pointed out.

Julie had looked forever before settling on the small colonial nestled beneath a blanket of ancient maple trees. Peaceful and warm, it was everything she thought a home should be.

"Although it's in kind of a stodgy neighborhood," Rhonda added.

"Hey," Julie said defensively, "I love my neighborhood."

"Well, sure, it's safe. And homey. And quiet. If you like that sort of thing."

"I do," Julie said even as Rhonda continued talking.

"All your neighbors are old enough to be my grandparents. They consider a game of gin rummy a really wild time. The men wear fedoras and the women wear scarves over their hair on a breezy day. I'll bet half of them use walkers."

"Your point being?"

"Well, just that an eligible young woman like yourself should probably live someplace where she can meet other eligible types. Like guys. Or maybe some other single girlfriends. Hell, I doubt you could even come up with a tennis partner on your street."

"I don't play tennis."

"See what I mean?"

"For your information," Julie said, "there's that new guy up the street. Remember? I told you about him. Early thirties. Really good looking."

Rhonda snapped her fingers. "I'd almost forgotten about him, but that 'really good-looking' part jogged my memory."

"Typical," Julie mumbled.

"I believe I set a goal for you, young lady, did I not? Have you found a way to meet him yet?"

"No," Julie said, shaking her head. She remembered the other day when he'd been out raking leaves as she'd driven by on her way home from the shop. He'd been wearing a big, cuddly-looking hooded sweatshirt with a pleasantly snug pair of faded blue jeans. His thick, dark hair had looked as if it might need a trim, but Julie liked it that way.

"If he were right across the street or something, it would be easier," Julie said. "But he's too far away for natural interaction."

"Didn't you say he had a kid?" Rhonda asked.

"Yeah, a little boy. Really cute."

"But no wife, right?"

"I don't think so. I've never seen anyone there besides the dad and the child, except maybe a grandma once, and there's usually only one car in the driveway."

Rhonda cast an approving glance toward Julie. "Good work scoping out the situation."

"Well, I wouldn't want to let you down, coach," Julie said wryly.

"Maybe you can get chummy with the kid," Rhonda suggested. "Give him some candy or something."

But Julie shook her head. "You know that no self-respecting child would take candy from a stranger."

"Yes. But..." Rhonda said, holding a finger triumphantly in the air, "tomorrow night is Halloween. The one night when that rule doesn't apply. It's your big chance."

Julie tilted her head. An interesting thought, but certainly not something that could be counted on. "Yeah, well," she said, "he'll have to come to me. I'm not roaming the streets looking for the kid. And for all we know, the little boy will be with the missing mother tomorrow night and the dad will stay home and hand out candy."

Rhonda's eyes sparkled lecherously in the car's darkness. "Well then, I say you just put on this nifty little witch dress again, march up to his door, say 'Trick or treat', and pray to God that he says 'Trick'."

Julie laughed and rolled her eyes. "I'm going to feel uncomfortable enough in this dress in front of a lot of people I don't know, let alone parading around in it for my neighbors to see."

Rhonda looked displeased, her eyes focused back out on the road. "You're still not over this yet?"

"Over what yet?"

"This Halloween party-witch dress phobia."

Julie took a deep breath and thought about the question. She considered adapting a new, brave, bold attitude, considered tossing all her adolescent hang-ups right out the window and starting her social life completely over. But she failed with a sigh. "No."

Rhonda turned down a side street and slowed the car, peering out the windshield at the street numbers on the mailboxes. Knowing that they must have arrived, Julie began to feel quivery with nerves.

"There it is," Rhonda announced, pointing.

Before them stood an average-sized ranch house with cars packed into the yard like sardines, and sandwiched into every nook and cranny in the driveway and up and down the narrow residential street. "I'm especially not over it now," Julie added, her stomach churning.

"You're really that worried about walking into a party with me?" Rhonda asked.

"Considering that I won't know a soul besides you, and that I'm wearing this, this…oddly-fitting dress and this ridiculous hat, and that I hate parties, and that I…I…"

"I have a theory about you," her friend quietly imparted.

Julie blinked and tilted her head slightly. "Oh?"

"I know you like to socialize with grandmas and other blue-hair types, but I have a suspicion that deep down inside you're really not as big a stick in the mud as you like to appear."

"You don't think so, huh?"

"No," Rhonda replied, scanning the street for a parking spot. "You liked Patrick, after all, and even though he was a jerk, he *was* a lot of fun."

Julie sighed wistfully. "True. He was." More fun than she could handle, actually.

"In fact, I think that's the whole problem," Rhonda explained. She wedged the car into a small space along the curb as she spoke. "I think Patrick scared you away from fun. Every time you'd loosen up and let yourself do anything fun with him, he'd turn it into something dirty, or he'd let you down in some way, and you'd end up feeling bad. It's a lot less risky hanging out with senior citizens, I suppose."

Julie tried to defend herself. "That's not why I hang around with senior citizens. All my neighbors are older. Most of my customers are, too. Can I help that?"

Rhonda ignored her, continuing. "I have an idea for you, for tonight, if you're interested."

Julie figured she didn't have anything to lose. And now, with her actual entrance to the party looming so near, she felt desperate. "Out with it," she said.

"Don't be so *you* tonight."

"What on earth does *that* mean?"

"In fact, don't be you at all. Be someone else."

"Like who?" Julie asked.

"Be me. Or anyone else you consider fun-loving and an all around good time. Make someone up. None of these people know you. And none of them will ever see you again. So be someone in your imagination, someone you've always wanted to be. And just to help you along," she added, reaching into the back seat, into the same shopping bag from which Julie's costume had emerged, "wear this."

Julie looked up expecting to see the ugly witch's nose in Rhonda's hand again, but instead her friend held a small black velvet mask, the kind that covered the eyes and the top of the nose, with an elastic strap to hold it on.

Julie studied the mask and bit her lip nervously.

"Be dark and mysterious," Rhonda prodded her. "Be the beautiful, unknown woman in the sexy dress with the hidden past. It'll drive guys wild."

Julie swallowed. "But is that what I want? To drive guys wild?"

"You're a healthy, red-blooded American woman," Rhonda reminded her. "Of course that's what you want."

And when she didn't answer right away, her friend kept going, clearly sensing her hesitation. "Come on—don't just be Julie the insecure antique dealer with the cute house on the quiet street tonight."

"But who should I be?" she asked again cautiously.

After which Rhonda thought for a moment, then got that familiar and wild look in her eyes. "Be…Electra, the mysterious woman visiting from New York. Be a big city fashion model."

"That's a *stupid* name and I'm too old and too curvy to be a model."

"It's a *cool* name, and these guys aren't brain surgeons—they won't know the toddler toothpick trends in modeling."

"I'll wear the mask," Julie conceded, taking it from Rhonda. "But the model stuff isn't gonna fly."

"Whatever," Rhonda said. "You make up the story when they start asking. But I promise you, that mask is going to be a man-catcher."

"Sort of like a woman who has to swim across the Amazon attaching fish food to herself, isn't it?" Julie asked as she removed her hat to slip the velvet mask over her head.

"Well, you don't have to wear it if you don't want to," Rhonda pointed out.

But the mask was already in place. And it felt soft and warm against Julie's skin. Strangely protective. She liked it. "How do I look?" she asked, turning to face Rhonda in the car.

And Rhonda smiled. "Sexy. And mysterious. Like any good man-catcher should."

Julie exited the car feeling uncharacteristically confident and even a smidge aloof. A fresh, cool breeze stirred around her, rustling the limbs in the trees and the dead leaves on the ground. She pulled her hat down snugly to keep it from blowing away.

Following Rhonda and her small red negligee through the maze of cars toward the front door, she wondered if she could actually pull this off. And her heartbeat grew faster as Rhonda pressed one bright red fingernail to the doorbell. She reached up to touch the comforting velvet of her mask again, like making a last desperate grab at a security blanket.

With butterflies dancing in her stomach, she waited nervously—until the door burst wide open. Loud music and wild laughter poured out into the yard from behind the man in the skeleton suit who stood before them.

He flashed a wide smile through a face painted with black and white makeup. "Come on in, ladies," he said, "and feel free to jump my bones."

Chapter Two

RHONDA RELEASED A laugh and Julie sucked in her breath, quite glad she wasn't the one standing closest to the letch at the door. His skeleton suit fit skin tight from neck to toe, a giant leotard with the appropriate bones sewn onto the front and back in glowing white. In theory, it was a great costume, but Julie thought it a little snug, especially on a guy. Still, she couldn't quite take her eyes off it, either.

"Watch out," Rhonda said playfully to the skeleton guy. "I have a pitchfork and I'm not afraid to use it."

The skeleton grinned. "Ooo," he said, "kinky."

Rhonda moved inside, appearing just as confident and perky as usual, floating through the room like the social butterfly she'd always been. Her eyes were bright, her smile pretty, and everything about her screamed fun.

Julie, on the other hand, felt as if she were preparing to run a gauntlet. Every person in the room felt like an enemy, or an opponent. Either way, all were definitely to be avoided. She immediately looked forward to the moment when she could find a nice quiet corner to hide in while she waited for this whole event to be over.

"And what do we have here?" Skeleton Guy asked, his probing eyes suddenly glued to Julie as she crossed the threshold. "A cute little Witchiepoo. Hey," he said, as if in search of a revelation, "what show was that on?"

"*H.R. Pufnstuf*," Julie replied evenly, naming the old 70s kids show as she tried to move past him.

"Impressive," he said, probably because it had aired long before either of them had been born. "But you're much better looking than her."

"No green-tinted face," she said shortly.

His mouth spread into a grin. "You can put a spell on me anytime. What's your name?"

For a flash of a second, Julie tried very hard to think of a mysterious name, of some special identity to assume, something better than Rhonda's silly Electra. But who could she be?

"Excuse me," she said instead, when nothing came to mind. It seemed the only sensible answer, or lack thereof. She took a step forward, anxious to get away from the guy in the tight-fitting costume.

"Wait," he said, touching her arm.

She looked up at him, thankful for her mask.

"Aren't you going to tell me your name?"

Think mysterious. Think, think, think. But she *wasn't* mysterious and she didn't know *how to be* mysterious, so her mind stayed blank. She silently shook her head.

"All right then, Witchiepoo," he said with a smile. And it seemed like almost a *kind* smile, although it was hard to read beneath that glaringly painted face. It made her wonder if he could see how frightened her eyes were behind the velvet mask, or if it was instead doing what she had hoped, hiding her emotions as well as her face.

Like a child excused, she turned to move away from him through the room. Paper spiders and ghosts hung from light fixtures on the ceiling, and fake cobwebs draped from lamps, bookcases, and picture frames. Julie shuddered at the multitude of people in one small space, remembering all over again why she hated parties.

She peered about the room searching for Rhonda, but not a devil in sight.

Only, wait, no, there were suddenly *three* devils in sight. Make that four. One was a guy, complete with a big red cape, his face and body painted entirely red from head to toe. His red plastic pitchfork was actually large enough to look dangerous.

Suddenly a hand came to rest on Julie's shoulder— and she jumped.

"Geez, would you relax?" Rhonda said. "How are you doing so far?"

"Not very well. I feel terribly out of place."

"Well, you *should* feel great. I don't see any other witches at all. And I, for one, feel terribly unoriginal. Have you seen all these tacky devils? The girl with the sequins? Have you gotten a good look at her? She's even glued big red sequin flames onto her face. I think it's a little much. Maybe they won't come off and she'll have to wear them for life. I look sexier than her, don't you think?"

"Yes," Julie replied. "But that's not necessarily a compliment. It just means you're wearing a much skimpier outfit."

"And did you see that man-devil?" Rhonda asked.

Julie nodded.

"Did you get a load of the pitchfork on that guy? I might have to go spar with him."

And Julie tried to smile, but she couldn't. She felt far too uncomfortable. Even as Rhonda talked a blue streak, Julie could sense the eyes upon them. Every manner of monster, cowboy, caveman, and clown perused them with lecherous eyes, made even more potentially frightening by the fact that their identity was hidden—Julie could tell nothing about them from their appearance except that they liked a good Halloween party and, from the indication given by their not-shy eyes, that they weren't gay. Julie and Rhonda were the new arrivals on the scene, two girls who no one knew, and they were obviously good fodder for conversation.

"Everyone's staring at us," Julie whispered.

And Rhonda smiled triumphantly. "I know. We must look pretty good."

"I never should have worn this dress," Julie muttered.

"How many times do I have to tell you to relax? This is going to be a great time, I promise. After all, we're not the only ones looking good around here. This is a veritable feast of men."

Though Julie's eyes went wide with disbelief.

"Rhonda, you can't even see their faces!"

"A face isn't everything," Rhonda pointed out. "For instance, that skeleton dude that answered the door—he's not exactly skin and bones."

"His outfit is a little tight if you ask me."

"Mmm mmm good," Rhonda murmured as if auditioning for a Campbell's Soup commercial. "With a body like that, the man has every right to wear his clothes as tight as he wants."

Julie said nothing, but thought again of Skeleton Guy. Rhonda was right. He was undeniably well built. His arms and legs had all the right muscles—big without being he-man big—and he looked appropriately hard and soft in all the right places.

Which made a shamefully lascivious thought pop into her head. What if he got hard…there? Nothing would hide it. Just that thin black fabric. She tried to push the thought away, but it made her feel horribly warm all through her dress before she could do anything to stop it.

Her mind was forced back to the party, however, when a hand grabbed onto Rhonda's shoulder and spun her around. A bawdy saloon girl decked out in a garish shade of purple began to twitter and chat with wild gesticulations and animated eyes. A riverboat gambler stood by the saloon girl's side. Julie figured these must be Rhonda's old neighbors.

Julie waited politely behind Rhonda, soon to realize that the room was far too loud for proper introductions.

Then, before Julie knew it, she heard the saloon girl's muted voice saying, "There's somebody I want you to meet," just before she yanked Rhonda away through the crowd.

By the time Julie realized what was happening, Rhonda had already disappeared into the next room. The crowd was too dense to move through comfortably, making it fruitless to follow, and Julie felt horribly stranded, but she took a deep breath and steeled herself. *Don't panic.* Then she tried to figure out some way not to appear as she was: frightened and alone. Standing by herself in the middle of a party was not her idea of…well, a party. "Oh bother," she mumbled beneath her breath.

"Winnie-the-Pooh," a voice said beside her.

And she looked up, wondering who knew that she'd unwittingly been quoting the storybook bear.

She nearly gasped, but held it in. It was Skeleton Guy. Looking even more muscular in that skin-tight outfit now that she'd allowed herself the opportunity to think about it. "Can I get you a drink, Witchiepoo?"

Her first thought was to decline. With or without that nice hard body, he was still the guy who had opened the door with an invitation to jump his bones. She knew it was just a skeleton joke, but it still made her uncomfortable.

Yet compared to all the other strangers in the room, his face seemed a friendly one. Even if she couldn't quite see what it looked like, bathed in white with black lines running around his eyes and mouth and entirely covering his nose, skeleton-style. He was the only person at the party who had spoken to her, and it only made sense to take advantage of that, rather than willingly remain stranded any longer.

"All right," she said softly.

"Follow me," he told her. Then he took her hand and led her through the room to a table covered with countless liquor bottles, soft drinks, a large punch bowl, and several stacks of orange and black plastic cups. His hand felt warm in hers, although the fabric of his costume covered it, extending completely over his fingers and toes for full skeleton effect. She wondered what his skin would feel like underneath.

"Here," he whispered, taking the witch's broom from her hand and placing it behind the table. "Let's stick your little Vroom-Broom back here for a while."

She couldn't help being as impressed as *he'd* originally been—that he'd remembered the name of Miss Witchiepoo's broom. Still, she asked, "Why?"

"To free up your hands." His raised eyebrows suggested some sexual connotation behind the words—even though he followed with something entirely different. "In case you want to dip into the pretzels while you're holding your drink. What would you like?"

Julie didn't want to get drunk in the too-crowded room, so she chose conservatively. "I'll just have some punch."

Skeleton Guy dipped two scoopfuls of punch into a

large orange cup, passing it her way, before filling his own glass with the same.

She took a sip, then grimaced. "What *is* this?"

"Rum punch," he said. "Straight from the islands. Probably a little heavy on the rum, though, if I know this crowd."

"You could say that," she affirmed, watching as he took a long swallow of his drink.

She tried another small sip, letting the warmth of the alcohol spread through her. And as she got used to it, she had to admit the punch was tasty. She tried not to let it remind her of her trip to Jamaica with Patrick, or of how he'd flirted with every other woman on the beach, or of the times she'd never even bothered to mention to him—the times she'd awakened in their hotel room in the middle of the night, alone.

But wait—what was she doing still thinking about Patrick? If nothing else, this party was supposed to take her mind off the jerk, so she worked to push her thoughts of him away.

Besides, she needed to concentrate on Skeleton Guy. His very presence made her nervous, so she had to stay sharp. She promised herself to drink slowly. She had to, or else risk…well, she wasn't exactly sure *what* she feared she'd be risking, but something about this guy, and this whole party, made her want to keep very alert.

"So, Witchiepoo," Skeleton Guy said, "what do you do?"

Simple question. *I'm an antique dealer. I have my own*

shop not far from here.

She wanted to say those words. Because she was proud of herself and her shop, and because it was a perfectly respectable vocation.

But it sounded so boring.

Not usually. Not if she were standing in a room full of middle-aged moms wearing warm fall sweaters and getting ready to redecorate their houses. But here, now, surrounded by all these obviously fun people, and with this very well-built skeleton staring her down, waiting for an answer, she just couldn't say the words. She couldn't be Julie the antique dealer. Besides, hadn't Rhonda told her to be someone new, someone different? And she was even wearing a mask to help perpetuate the fantasy.

"I'm a model," she spewed. Then she took a big drink of rum punch to help her figure out where she was going with this.

"A model?" he said, one eyebrow raising. "Cool. What do you model?"

She swallowed. What did she model? "Casualwear," she said. "Eveningwear," she added on impulse. "Sometimes bathing suits." *Sometimes bathing suits?* She threw back another gulp of her punch.

And Skeleton Guy grinned. He obviously liked bathing suits. "Bikinis?" he asked.

"Yes," she replied simply, still stunned at her own words.

"Ever model nude?" he asked with curious eyes and a playful smile.

"No," she told him, finally getting hold of herself. "Not my thing."

"Will you model for *me*?"

"Why? Are you a photographer?"

"No," he said, his grin widening, "but I could pretend to be if you were nude."

Julie felt her blood run cold. She knew he was only kidding; she knew she'd practically been asking for it. But something inside her prickled. Just who did this Skeleton Guy think he was? And she knew it was dumb to reprimand a man she'd just been openly flirting with, but she couldn't seem to stop herself. "That was out of line."

"It was?" he asked, obviously surprised at her reaction.

"Yes."

"How so?"

"You implied that I would take off my clothes for you when you don't even know me, or anything about me," she told him. "What gives you the right to speak to me that way?"

Skeleton Guy still looked taken aback, but then his expression relaxed into something calmer—and even smug. "What gives me the right?" he repeated. "*That dress* gives me the right."

A gasp escaped her. "What?"

"You shouldn't wear a dress like *that* to a party like *this* if you're so easily offended, Witchiepoo."

"And just what's wrong with my dress?" she demanded, knowing full well what was wrong with her dress, and also wondering just kind of a party *this* was.

"Nothing," he said. "You look great in it. But it puts ideas in a man's head. And when I see a girl in a dress that tight, I don't assume she's so sensitive. I mean, geez, I was just joking around, Witchiepoo. Don't get so mad."

"Quit calling me Witchiepoo," she shot back.

And he raised his bone-clad arms in a helpless gesture. "What am I supposed to call you then? You won't tell me your name."

"You don't have to call me anything," she informed him, "because this conversation is over."

With that, Julie turned on her heel and escaped through the crowd. Amazing how quickly she could get away from someone when she really wanted to, even in this tight sea of people. Although, despite her heart beating with nervous anger, she wasn't exactly sure why she'd wanted to get away from him so badly.

So he'd made a smart remark. Did that necessarily make him a rotten guy? Maybe she was just embarrassed now that he'd confirmed her suspicions about the dress. She knew she shouldn't have worn it and a glance down at her cleavage made her feel practically naked.

Was *everyone* looking at her like that, making assumptions about her, thinking she was the kind of girl you could talk dirty to? Had she suddenly turned into the type of woman Patrick had always wished her to be? Again, the irony of the situation struck her, and now, more than ever, she wanted to find that corner to hide in.

She moved briskly through the house looking for Rhonda. Where the hell had she gone? Seemed there were devils mingling everywhere, but none of them were her friend.

Roaming into a room that was devil-free, she quickly turned to leave. But before she could exit, a huge shadow moved into her path and she looked up to find a swarthy pirate, complete with a black eye-patch and filthy teeth. "Aye," he addressed her, "a fine wench ye be."

Scraggly and unshaven, he looked like he'd been at sea for years. And Julie wasn't in the mood for any more suggestive approaches. "Why don't you take a long walk off a short plank," she suggested, moving around him and back out into the hallway.

Where was Rhonda? She made her way into yet another mystery room to see that no devils in here looked like her, either. Julie had never felt so abandoned in her life and she resolved to kill her friend on sight.

Uh-oh. A grubby-looking cowboy sidled toward her and even as fast as she walked, she couldn't get past him. "Howdy there, little lady," he said, tipping his big white hat. "How's about me and you moseyin' over to the bar fer a shot o' red eye?"

"No thanks," she replied coolly, "but I may give you a *black* eye if you don't leave me alone."

God, this house is a maze. Exasperated, she had no other choice but to forge on. Locating Rhonda wouldn't solve all her party problems, but at least she'd have a companion, someone to stand next to, drink with, whisper to.

And murder.

Well, maybe she'd wait until *after* the party for that part.

The crowd gathered in the small kitchen was sparser than in the rest of the house, and Julie would have expected that to be a blessing, but it turned out to be a curse. The room was inhabited by only a handful of monster wannabes and it made her entry conspicuous. She felt the lecherous eyes immediately, but she refused to make eye contact as she bolted anxiously for the opposite doorway.

She attempted to look angry and unapproachable, just like she'd always heard a woman should do to ward off rapists. But she didn't see how the effort could ward off a rapist when it couldn't even ward off an aggressive guy wearing a Hawaiian shirt and a grass skirt, who moved toward her before she could get away.

"Pardon me," he said very politely. Then he removed a long chain of silk flowers from around his neck. "How would you like to get laid?"

She glared into a set of beady little eyes and replied firmly, "How would you like a nice Hawaiian Punch?" Then she swiftly escaped the room.

Julie's nerve-wracking tour of the house finally concluded when she realized she'd ended up back in the first room she'd left. And she was beginning to be more than a little sorry she'd stomped away from Skeleton Guy. Compared to the pirate and the cowboy, not to mention the beady-eyed beach boy, he seemed like a prince. Possibly almost like a friend. And even a slightly lewd friend was better than no friend at all. She realized that, despite his suggestive conversation, nothing he'd said or done had really made her feel threatened, and she couldn't say the same for the rest of those bozos, though it was more about the looks in their eyes than the things they'd actually said to her.

Finding her cup almost empty, she made her way back to the drink table for a refill. Lifting it to her lips, it turned out, gave her something to do, some purpose other than standing there staring blankly into the crowd while at the same time working madly not to make eye contact with anyone.

Then she eased through the throng of partygoers and finally found a comfortable place to stand, that proverbial safe corner she'd been dreaming about since the second she'd arrived. Wedging her body between a wooden bookcase and a large houseplant, she leaned back against the wall, taking a long sip of punch. She even reached up above her head and pulled at the fake cobwebs draped over the top corner of the shelves so that they hung down over her face a little, just hoping to blend in and not be noticed.

Once situated in her private little space, she got her first opportunity to study the crowd. In addition to the tribe of mingling devils, she spied a mummy, a werewolf, several non-specific monsters, and a whole host of grim reapers all standing around—drinks in one hand, scythes in the other. A half dozen people stood in neat, orderly formation, each encased in a circle of tin and all tied to each other with plastic; they had come as a six-pack of beer. And one obviously drunken man had dressed as a bag of garbage and roamed among the women asking who wanted to take him outside.

Julie found it much easier to laugh and enjoy people's creativity when she wasn't so worried about fitting in. She only started to feel self-conscious again when she narrowed her study on some of the other females at the party. A hula dancer with a coconut bra swished her grass skirt about the room, and a Playboy bunny with a fluffy white tail wiggled it. A couple of flappers smoked and flirted provocatively. All those damn sexy devils flitted around poking people with their pitchforks. And a belly dancer with a coin imbedded in her navel demonstrated her dancing skills.

Okay, maybe it wasn't so horrible to look a little sexy. Obviously she wasn't the only woman at the party dressed that way. Although she still felt the huge hat on her head was completely ridiculous and had to wonder if any guy could really find her attractive in it. Her self-doubt almost made her long for Skeleton Guy again. How odd that in one moment his comments had offended her, yet now she yearned for his admiration.

"Oh my God," she muttered beneath her breath, having just laid eyes on the most outrageous costume in the room. Lady Godiva. The tall, shapely woman wore a flesh-colored catsuit that made her appear to be clothed in nothing at all besides high heels and a voluminous wig that hung well past her waist. She stood close enough for Julie to see that locks of fake hair covered her breasts and even dipped to creatively shelter the spot between her legs.

And seeing Lady Godiva quickly put Julie back in her right mind. Sexy and showy could sometimes go too far. Of course, compared to *that* chick, Julie looked like a nun, tight dress or not—but who needed the kind of admiration skimpy clothes bought?

Take that, Patrick. A simple dress had not succeeded in transforming her into the kind of girl you could talk dirty to. In fact, it left her feeling as it had every other time in her life when she'd tried wearing something provocative. Self-conscious and uncomfortable.

"Hey, how ya doing?"

Julie knew the voice belonged to Skeleton Guy. She lifted her eyes hopefully when the very sound of it warmed her.

It took her a moment to realize, though, that he wasn't talking to her. Lady Godiva was the recipient of his attention now.

Mortified, Julie gingerly squeezed her body out from between the shelves and the plant and made for the bathroom. She didn't want to let Skeleton Guy see her standing there looking lost and forlorn, hiding behind a cobweb—and she wasn't exactly in the mood to watch two people in spandex drool over each other.

Once in the bathroom, she stared at herself in the mirror. *What am I doing here?* She didn't know these people, so why on earth should she care about impressing them?

A model? She'd had to take Rhonda's silly advice and say she was a model? She didn't even *want* to be a model. And she didn't want to be a witch and she didn't want to be sexy! She didn't want to be anything that Patrick would have pushed her to be.

Julie rolled her eyes at herself in the mirror. Patrick! Why was he still in her head? *He's engaged. To the girl he cheated on you with. And he's a jerk. Familiar to you, yes, but a loser on all other counts. Get over him. Get back out there and give Skeleton Guy a chance. Give that sleazy Lady Godiva a run for her money.* Rhonda had been right— that dress wasn't low-cut for nothin'.

Julie powdered her nose, touched up her lipstick, and emerged from the bathroom a new witch. She strolled quickly and confidently to the room where she'd last seen her Skeleton Guy flirting with Lady Godiva.

But when she got there, most of the people that had occupied the space before had surprisingly vanished.

Her attention was drawn momentarily to the television in the corner. She hadn't even realized it was on when the room had been so crammed full of people, but now a newsbreak reported that escaped mental patient and suspected serial killer, Daryl Dukes, had been linked to yet another local murder. *Hell of a thing to have to think about this close to Halloween.* She shivered, then reached down to turn off the TV. No one was watching it anyway.

Then she remembered her slightly less tragic predicament: how lost and forlorn she was, how stupid she felt, and the fact that Skeleton Guy and Lady Godiva were suddenly nowhere to be seen.

"Action's in there," an overweight priest told her, apparently noticing her befuddlement. He pointed toward a closed door across the hallway.

Curious, Julie freshened her drink again, then headed toward the indicated door—which she guessed led to one of the bedrooms. It wasn't hard to hear the muffled sounds of the crowd inside—they were cheering and whistling. She wondered what the *action* was.

She cautiously reached down to turn the knob—when the door opened of its own accord, letting an explosion of music and whistles escape into the hall. Julie glanced up to find herself face to face with Skeleton Guy—they both stopped abruptly to avoid crashing into each other, but their bodies lingered less than an inch apart.

He looked surprised to see her. Then he put both big hands firmly on her shoulders and backed her out of the doorway. Her heart skipped a beat at his touch.

"I don't think you want to go in there," he informed her.

"Why not?" She tried to peek over his shoulder, but he was too tall. "What's going on?" Another loud whistle came from within the room.

He reached back to close the door behind them, shutting out most of the noise. "Somebody hired a stripper," he said.

The news grounded Julie in place. She supposed that was what Skeleton Guy had meant earlier when he'd referred to the gathering as *this kind of party*.

"Oh," she mumbled. "Then how come *you're* not in there?"

He shook his head slightly, and repeated the answer she'd given him earlier, about nude modeling. "Not my thing."

And she just stared at him, half in shock, half in disbelief.

"Don't look at me like that, Witchiepoo," he told her. "It doesn't mean I'm gay or anything. It's just not what I'm into, okay?"

"I'm sorry," she said. "I'm just a little shocked."

"Why?"

"Well, you seem *exactly* like the kind of guy who would be into that sort of thing."

"So you're stereotyping me just because of my jokes with you earlier."

"Just like you stereotyped me because of my dress."

He shrugged. "Fair enough." Then he glanced around her. "So are you here alone or what?"

Julie blushed. "I came with a friend, but I haven't seen her since we walked in the door."

"Oh yeah," he said, snapping his fingers. "I remember. The kinky devil."

"Right."

"Well, you don't look like you're having a very good time. Despite that dress, I'm beginning to think you're not the wild party type."

She put her finger on her nose, the universal charades sign for correct.

"So what type *are* you?" he asked.

The question made her nervous and she reached to fidget with the plastic spiders hanging at her neck. "The stay-at-home type," she finally admitted. "Pretty boring, huh?"

"Not necessarily. You can have a lot of fun at home." He grinned at his own statement, which added to her nerves even more. She feared he was on the verge of asking her out. Or in, for some kind of pizza/movie/sexual encounter type date.

Which she knew shouldn't be a scary thing. But it was, with or without the sex part. For one thing, she couldn't even see the guy's face. And for another, she hadn't had a first date of any kind in over three years. She wasn't sure she was ready. She wasn't sure she would *ever* be.

"I guess modeling is pretty tiring work, huh?" he asked then. "Probably why you don't like to go out a lot."

"I'm not a model," she blurted out.

"What?" he asked, wide-eyed.

Then she shook her head, confused with her own

motivations. "I just said that because…" Because why? "Because I'm really just an antique dealer and I didn't think that would sound very intriguing." She felt her cheeks go warm.

When his gaze turned strange, thoughtful, she wished she knew what he was thinking. If he was angry with her for lying. Or merely thought she was stupid for lying. Either prospect seemed dire.

"I like antiques," he said softly.

"You do?"

"Sure. I mean, I don't know much about them, but I certainly have nothing against them."

"Yeah?"

"And I have a desk," he went on, "from my grandmother, that's been passed down through the family for generations. So I even *own* an antique."

"What period?" she asked.

"I don't know," he said, shaking his head. "Around the Civil War? Maybe you could come take a look at it sometime."

Julie's heart rate increased ten-fold. "I have a boyfriend," she spewed at him, panicked.

"What?"

"I'm engaged," she lied. "And I know he wouldn't like the idea of me going to a man's house like that. Even if it was just on business."

"Oh," he said. "Okay."

But Lord, why had she started spurting lies like that? One mention of seeing him again and she'd simply fallen apart. Her defense mechanisms had taken over before she could even think. She'd cleared up one lie merely to replace it with another, and now the awkward silence hung over them like a heavy cloud that nearly stifled her breathing.

Skeleton Guy sighed and Julie continued to feel ridiculous. "So," he said, "where *is* this guy? Why isn't he here with you?"

She swallowed. "I promised my friend, the kinky devil, that I'd come with her. But my fiancé, he's…not into parties. So he's at home."

"Waiting for your return."

She nodded nervously.

"Lucky guy," he mumbled.

"What?" she whispered, her heart pounding in her chest.

"Nothing," he said. Then he changed the subject. "I'm sure he wouldn't have wanted you to come if he'd known what a wild party it would be."

"Probably not," she said, thinking of Patrick, knowing that he'd be the *first* to drag her to a wild party, and that if he were here right now he'd probably be in the bedroom dancing with the stripper, more than likely removing his own clothing as well as hers.

"Hey," said a familiar voice behind Julie—and a sudden relief washed over her. Just before she remembered her silent vow of murder.

"Hey yourself," she sternly replied, turning to face Rhonda. "Where on earth have you been?"

"Sorry," she said, her eyes apologizing more than her tone of voice. "I just got caught up talking to people."

Julie nodded. "Figures."

"Skeleton dude!" Rhonda looked past Julie to greet him in her best surfer voice. She'd obviously been dipping into the rum punch, too.

"Kinky devil!" he greeted her back.

"Anybody jump your bones yet?"

"Nope," he said, his hands held out in pretend despair. "I've been trying—" he offered a glance toward Julie, "—but I can't get any takers."

"*Hell* if I know why," Rhonda said. "I think you're a *devil* of a good looking man."

"Not too bony?" he asked.

"Not at all. For a man made of bones, you have a fabulous body. Right, Jules?"

"Right," Julie nervously replied, deciding she would make Rhonda's death a slow and torturous one.

"Listen, you guys," Rhonda said, "a bunch of people are going to leave and go to some haunted house way out in the country. Doesn't that sound like a *devil* of a good time?"

"Sure," Skeleton Guy said. "Maybe somebody'll jump my bones in *there*. You think so, Witchiepoo?" His eyes upon her were warm but fraught with a sweet sheepishness that nearly drowned her.

And no words would come, so Julie merely nodded.

"Witchiepoo," Rhonda repeated, hearing it for the first time. "That's one *hell* of a cute name. Now grab your broom and let's get out of here. They're loading up the cars out front."

Julie glumly followed Rhonda and Skeleton Guy toward the front door. She didn't get the idea she had any choice about this haunted house business. Yet she didn't have the strength to fight it. Would this horrid night never end?

Still, a tiny piece of her heart knew she wasn't quite ready to say goodbye to Skeleton Guy yet. So maybe, just maybe, this was meant to be. She took a detour to pick up her broom where he'd stashed it by the drink table earlier, then headed out into the darkness.

Stepping outside, Julie felt surreal. The rum was getting to her, making her unsteady, making the ground feel strange and squishy beneath her feet. Still, it wasn't hard to spot Skeleton Guy. His bones glowed in the dark. And it also wasn't hard to spot Rhonda. She was bellowing "Devil With the Blue Dress" into the handle of her pitchfork as if it were a microphone. The bad thing was that they were both moving in opposite directions.

"Hey Witchiepoo," Skeleton Guy yelled across the lawn-turned-parking lot.

She looked up anxiously, thinking maybe he was going to ask her to ride in the same car with him. The notion made her feel sixteen again, but she didn't mind. Romance had seemed so much easier then.

His distant smile on her was playful—but instead of issuing an invitation, he said, "Watch where you're going. You're trampling those mums to death."

And she looked down, mortified to find herself standing in a bed of golden fall mums, now crushed beneath her feet. She must be drunker than she realized. She felt too stupid to even acknowledge his words, and her eyes stayed glued to her shoes.

"Come on, Jules," Rhonda sang out then, suddenly at her side, grabbing onto one black dress sleeve. Then she swiftly dragged Julie into a car with Darth Vader, a biker chick, and two ghosts before she could even think about protesting.

Once closed up inside the car, Julie gazed out the window, feeling strangely lost and alone again, even with Rhonda next to her. And she touched her hand softly to the pane, peering into the distance as Skeleton Guy climbed into a fast-looking car with Lady Godiva.

Chapter Three

JULIE HATED HAUNTED houses. What fun people saw in being scared she'd never understood. And she especially didn't understand it when the car she rode in pulled up outside the creepiest-looking old house she'd ever seen. She couldn't believe she was expected to go inside it.

They'd driven for at least half an hour up and down myriad winding roads she didn't recognize, leaving every ounce of suburbia far behind, and now faced this sagging, horrid house, the only house in sight, out in the middle of nowhere.

A thick cover of trees behind the house made its shape hard to discern. Full of sharp eaves and topped with two intricately shaped turrets, the entire structure appeared a dull gray in the moonlight. Julie shivered as she exited the car, Rhonda tumbling out behind her. "Ooo, spooky," Rhonda said. Then her focus changed and she started belting out her own special version of "Devil Went Down to Georgia".

Julie tapped her on the arm, halting her friend's song. "I don't think I'm going inside," she said.

"What? Why not?"

"I'd just rather wait out here, that's all."

"Oh," Rhonda said, "I forgot. You don't like haunted houses."

Julie nodded in confirmation, although she felt like the biggest loser alive. She didn't like parties, she didn't like aggressive men, she didn't like haunted houses—why did Rhonda even bother with her?

"Come on, Jules. It won't be bad. It'll be fun. You'll see."

Julie gazed up at the big house in the distance. It would be nice to be like Rhonda, nice to search out fun and adventure. But she simply didn't want to, and she felt too set in her ways to fight it. "No, that's okay. I'll be fine here. You go ahead."

"Are you sure?" Rhonda asked, pleading one last time.

And Julie was about to nod when something caught the corner of her eye. She glanced to her right to see Skeleton Guy's bones glowing in the darkness and her heartbeat quickened. She couldn't see Lady Godiva anywhere—but her spirits sank all over again when the woman's brackish laughter bit into the air.

"I changed my mind," Julie said without warning. "I'll go."

The words stopped Rhonda dead in her tracks. "You will?"

"Yes," Julie told her. "You're right. It won't be bad. It'll be fine. And I think it's about time I conquered a haunted house. Don't you?"

"Definitely," Rhonda said. Julie could see her knowing smile, clearly illumined by a golden moon overhead. "And maybe you'll even jump somebody's bones while you're at it."

"Why, whatever could you be talkin' about?" Julie asked in her best Scarlett O'Hara voice, one hand poised on her chest.

"Maybe I *should've* let you wear my devil outfit," Rhonda told her. "Since I think there's hope for you yet."

Drawn back into reality by another peal of raucous laughter from Spandex Woman, Julie sighed. "Then again, how does one compete with a woman who came as a nude?"

Rhonda chuckled, but then her eyes narrowed in clearly devious thought. "You know, I've read that it entices men a lot more when a woman reveals some of the package without showing off the whole thing." And with that, she grabbed the skirt of Julie's dress with both hands and gave a firm tug downward, lowering the neckline nearly another inch.

"You're bad," Julie scolded her with half a smile.

"And you're catching on," Rhonda said.

The two women moved swiftly through the wide leaf-strewn yard to catch up with the rest of the group, congregating outside the door of the eerie old house. Julie's skin tingled with nerves and anticipation. *Thank God I drank the rum punch, or I'd never have the guts to go through with this.*

With entering the haunted house.

With the sudden pursuit of Skeleton Guy in which she seemed to be engaging.

But she didn't want to think about it too hard. She just wanted to go with the flow, be Rhonda-like for a change, and see what happened. Thinking of her drunkenness, though, she glanced down just to make sure she wasn't standing in anyone's mums or anything else she shouldn't be standing in.

"Sorry, ghouls and guys," Julie heard an Igor type at the front door announce as they approached, "but it's midnight. Time to close up."

In response, mutters of disgust wove through the freshly assembled party crowd.

"Come on, man," said a three-hundred-pound guy wearing an oversized baby diaper and a bonnet on his head. "Make an exception. We drove all the way from town for this."

"No can do." Igor shook his head. "Some of the monsters have already gone home. It's probably a ghost town in there. No pun intended," he added.

"We'll take what we can get," a seven-foot Frankenstein boomed from the back of the crowd in a mask-muffled voice. "It's hell riding in a car in this thing, and I want something for my trouble."

"Come on, baby," the biker chick purred, stepping forward to slide an arm around Igor's shoulder. "Haunted houses really rev me up, if you know what I mean. I'll make it worth your while."

A collective chuckle rippled over the crowd as Igor blushed and the biker chick pressed her leather-clad chest against him suggestively. Julie stood next to Darth Vader, whom she'd gathered was Biker Chick's husband—and as his normally heavy breathing grew even rougher, she hoped he wouldn't start a fight.

"All right, all right," Igor finally said. "Give me a minute to go inside and get everybody set up for one more group."

"Way to go, Igor!" Rhonda shouted, punching her red pitchfork into the air.

And Julie took a tiny step backward to avoid being jabbed in the face by it, only to hear an "Ow!" behind her.

She looked over her shoulder to see who she had stepped on, then struggled to suppress her gasp. She should have known. Skeleton Guy.

Her heart fluttered at his proximity—they stood mere inches apart.

But her hopes dropped when she realized that Lady Godiva remained right next to him. "Oops, sorry," she said.

"Watch those heels, Witchiepoo," he told her playfully. "They're killers."

She glanced down at *his* feet then to see he had worn a pair of hiking boots. Then she raised her eyes questioningly back to his face.

"Okay, so they don't really go with the outfit," he

said. "But I'm not really sure what's hot in skeleton footwear these days and this costume doesn't have any soles in the feet."

"Souls?" Rhonda said, spinning to join the conversation. "Did someone say something about souls? We devils are always in the market for them, you know. Have one for sale?"

Skeleton Guy grinned. "I've got two, but I'm keeping them. As long as Witchiepoo's wearing those pointy heels, I need them for protection."

"Yes, she and her heels can get pretty wild," Rhonda chimed.

"Oh can she now?" Skeleton Guy replied in an intrigued voice so sexy that Julie's skin rippled.

"The stories she could tell," Rhonda went on.

He eyed her with interest. "Is all this true, Witchiepoo? I thought you were the stay-at-home type."

"Well…" she began, having no idea what to say.

"Oh, I get it," he said. "You're one of those *Bewitched*-Samantha-Stevens types. Mild mannered homebody by day, riding around on broomsticks by night."

"Samantha never rode on broomsticks," Julie corrected him. "Or only in emergencies, anyway."

"Mmm," he said, nodding. "Must have been my adolescent imagination. You'd be surprised the things young boys dream about in bed."

Julie pulled in her breath, but looked into his eyes, trying to be brave and not shy away from the sexuality he so comfortably put out there.

"Sometimes older boys, too," he added then.

And she couldn't break her gaze on him. How she longed to see him, to get a look beneath the makeup that hid his face from her view. Was he as sexy as he seemed, as he sounded, as his body appeared? Was that possible? She grew warm wondering.

That was when Lady Godiva looped a flesh-colored arm around the bones at his elbow. "I bet older boys dream of better things than silly old witches," she said softly—and blood rose to Julie's cheeks.

Skeleton Guy turned to the flesh-colored nympho. "And just what do you think we dream about?"

The woman released another of those brash chuckles that chilled Julie's senses. "Well, I don't know what you dream about *now*, but after tonight I bet you dream about *me*." She walked her fingers up his glowing rib cage and Julie quickly turned back around, unwilling to watch a masqueraded seduction.

"Okay, folks," Igor announced, stepping back out on the rickety porch, "I made arrangements to squeeze one last group through. Watch your step. And pay Medusa right inside the door."

Julie watched as Biker Chick stepped forward to show her gratitude, circling Igor's shoulder with one arm as his hands slid easily around her waist. He looked to be more than a little infatuated with her leather and chains. Darth Vader surged ahead through the crowd then, nudging Biker Chick through the door, and whispering to Igor in his deep, breathy voice, "Touch her again and you'll wish the force was with you."

Julie followed Darth's lead and pushed through the crowd, too, anxious to get away from Skeleton Guy and his naked lady. She'd rather face every monster known to man than endure all the touchy-feely-giggly stuff that was bound to take place between the two of them inside the dark house. She sighed at the realization that he'd been right: someone *would* jump his bones in there. Only it wouldn't be her.

Julie clamped onto Rhonda's wrist and dragged her behind, but after paying their admission to a woman who wore a wig of rubber snakes, she shoved her friend in front of her. Rhonda seemed to enjoy warding off monsters with her pitchfork and Julie figured she could use all the protection she could get.

"Take that, and that!" Rhonda yelled when a mad scientist appeared from a darkened room, coming at her with a plastic knife. She jabbed her fake pitchfork into his arm.

"Hey, quit sticking me with that thing!" the scientist said in shock, pulling back from her.

"Obviously not used to people who fight back," Rhonda said proudly to Julie over her shoulder.

Julie held onto Rhonda's glittering red devil tail, trusting her to guide them through. They passed by a torture chamber filled with haggard people in tattered clothes, covered with blood. They then moved through an equally bloody hospital scene and onto a room where ghosts flickered on the wall before the live ones actually leaped out.

Next came a woodsy room with lots of trees and greenery, and two or three howling werewolves who each got a jab of the red fork when they came near. Still, Julie had been touched by more than one monster's hand and she grew increasingly anxious to get out of the house.

When they stepped into a scene from hell complete with heat lamps, flames, and red devils, Rhonda stopped. "My people," she said like an alien returning to the mother ship.

"Would you move it?" Julie whispered in her ear, giving her friend a shove. "I want to get out of here."

"But I'm digging that guy," Rhonda said over her shoulder, pointing to a red, sharp-eared demon in the corner of the hot, gleaming room.

Again, Julie was confused about how Rhonda could be so easily attracted to men whose faces she couldn't really see.

Okay, so she was experiencing some attraction to Skeleton Guy. But at least she'd spoken to him. At least he seemed to have a personality—and possibly a cute one at that, once she'd begun to get used to it.

The demon in the corner, however, was a complete and total stranger who wore a hideous grin that practically curled Julie's toes. "His skin is bright red," Julie pointed out to her friend.

"I know," Rhonda whispered. "It's scary and mysterious. And it's really sort of turning me on."

"What?" Julie asked in disbelief.

"Just one of many common female fantasies," Rhonda informed her, again slipping into her documentary tone. "Being with someone whose identity stays secret."

Rhonda worked to make eye contact with the demon while Julie watched and wondered what it was like to live in Rhonda's hedonistic world. Finally her she-devil friend let the moment end and, breaking the gaze, sauntered slowly toward the next room.

Once there, a coffin burst open and a vampire attacked Rhonda with a cry of, "I vant to suck your blood!" And then chaos ensued.

Rhonda tried to pull away, jabbing the slick-haired guy with her pitchfork several times only to have him respond with, "Ooo, she likes to play rough."

A second vampire, one that had come with the party crowd, suddenly rushed forward from somewhere behind, his black cape spreading majestically behind him as he prepared for rescue. He punched the other vampire in the mouth, drawing real blood when the first Dracula's fang cut a lip. Then vampire number two scooped a shaken and grateful Rhonda up into his arms.

Julie realized, however, that much of Rhonda's fear had been fabricated when she pulled the rescuing vampire into a deep, hot kiss, fangs and all, producing a few yips and yells from those who witnessed it. And as Julie found herself wondering what it felt like to have those pointy fangs grinding into her lips, she began to think maybe she *did* understand just a hint of what

Rhonda had been saying before. Maybe there really *was* something alluring about being intimate with someone you couldn't quite see. She stirred warmly below and her thoughts returned to Skeleton Guy.

Who was probably somewhere groping Lady Godiva. Yuck.

She trudged on to the next room, hoping it would be the last one before this ridiculous night ended. As she took a careful step down, she said a silent prayer. *Please let me be outside now.*

But no. And not only was she not outside—wherever she was, the floor was moving. A mind-numbing strobe light blinked in a hideous fashion that made her instantly dizzy. Everyone in the room stumbled and fell into each other, and most were laughing. Not Julie, though. She struggled not to crumble in frustration.

She caught a glimpse of Rhonda and her vampire hanging all over each other, giggling like the rest. And another look around the disorienting room revealed Skeleton Guy and Lady Godiva—she clung to him as if for dear life as he tried to maneuver the floor. The entire crowd had made its way into the room now, but no one had yet found a way out.

"Over there," Skeleton Guy announced a moment later, his voice overriding the laughter. His glowing hand pointed the way.

She practically ran toward the exit, praying she wouldn't fall and be trampled, wanting out of that room worse than she'd possibly ever wanted out of anyplace in her life.

"Made it," she whispered to herself when her feet found solid ground again.

"Up, up, up," a ghastly figure sang out. It stood before her directing them with one long, thin, E.T.-like finger. Not even a moment to regain her senses. And unfortunately, the ghoul pointed toward a set of steps, which meant the horrendous trip wasn't even close to a conclusion. She actually considered straying from the pack, trying to find her own way out, but on second thought, that seemed like suicide. So she slowly climbed the stairs, very sorry to have ended up first in line.

She halted abruptly at the landing, though, the air before her suddenly pitch black. The person behind her, not anticipating her stop, bumped gently into her back—and she glanced over her shoulder at a glowing white skeleton face. "Oh," she breathed. He felt so warm pressing against her.

"Sorry," he murmured. He seemed not to realize it was her. But that was understandable—the darkness was overwhelming.

"This way," an eerie voice called. And a light began to blink on and off in the distance, down the hallway, and an invisible black curtain lifted. Julie eased cautiously forward past the curtain into a dimly lit room, wishing she had Rhonda's pitchfork, wishing…she had the simple courage to take Skeleton Guy's hand.

A man with a chainsaw leaped before her then, his eyes lit crazily as he pulled the cord to start the engine, sending sickly white smoke to waft through the air accompanied by the hideous sound. She caught sight of dismembered bodies lying about the room behind him, all covered in blood, along with a few spare arms and legs. One of the bodies suddenly came to life—an armless, legless guy lying on the floor muttering, "Help me. Please help me."

And Julie stopped cold. She couldn't explain, even to herself, the consuming horror that rattled all the way to her bones. Terror grounded her, leaving her unable to move, and all she could see were those crazy eyes bearing down on her.

Skeleton Guy bumped into her from behind again, obviously not having expected her to stop in the middle of the room. He was still warm. And solid. And the very feel of his body behind hers was somehow comforting, even in the midst of her paralyzing fear.

The maniac with the chainsaw started waving it around then, coming toward her—and she finally found the will to move, or *it* found *her*. She instinctively turned to flee, only to end up in Skeleton Guy's sturdy arms.

"Hey there," he said, his voice soft and gentle, his arms coming tenderly around her, "it's all right, Witchie-epoo. It's just pretend."

She looked wildly up into his eyes, seeing for the first time how brown they were, how deep and inviting. "But what if it's real?" she squeaked, wishing she could calm her frantic voice. Her fingers clawed against the white ribs on his chest as she savored the warmth of his embrace.

"It's not," he said. "I promise."

"But, but—" The sound of the chainsaw came closer, tensing every muscle in her body with stark fear—she knew it was right behind her and that she couldn't get away.

Then Skeleton Guy spoke gruffly. "Back off," he told the chainsaw-wielding nut.

But Julie could still feel the guy breathing down her neck.

"Did you hear me?" Skeleton Guy said. "I told you to back off and let the lady pass."

That was when she heard the chainsaw and its owner finally depart across the room. She continued staring into the glowing ribs before her, though, unable to look up, fearful that he would see the tears that had escaped her eyes.

"Go on now," he whispered softly. "It's okay."

Without glancing up, Julie turned and moved briskly through the room to what she hoped would be safety. But how could she feel safe—without those strong arms to hold her? The sudden lack of his touch left her with an intense emptiness, and despite all her feelings of loneliness at the party and at so many other times in her life, she didn't think she'd ever felt quite as alone as she suddenly felt in that strange moment without Skeleton Guy's protection.

Again, she found herself not outside, not returned to anyplace rendering safety or assurance—but located in a strange room that seemed not to have an exit. Instead it was covered with carnival mirrors. In one she looked fat. In another she appeared thin. In all of them she was tear-stained.

She could hear the renewed terror back in the chainsaw room and knew she wouldn't be alone for long—so she rushed to wipe her tears away before anyone else came in.

Soon the small room filled with people, yet Julie still felt alone. Where had Skeleton Guy gone? She'd expected him to be right behind her, but she didn't see him anywhere. Rhonda and her vampire made out in the center of the floor while Darth Vader and his biker chick seemed to be admiring how large her breasts looked in a corner mirror.

She finally found Skeleton Guy when she turned in the direction of Lady Godiva's loud whisper. The brash woman pressed against him, her arms wrapped around his neck. "Let's get out of here," she told him, "and go someplace where we can have some fun."

Julie felt sick and feared she might faint. She groped at the mirrors looking for escape—yet again it was Skeleton Guy who found the way out. She watched him push at a mirror, revealing a small doorway. Then he disappeared inside it, soon releasing a yelp that grew quickly hollow and distant but got the attention of everyone in the mirrored room, quieting them.

"Are you all right in there?" Rhonda yelled toward the black hole in the wall of mirrors.

"Yeah," he yelled back. "It's a slide."

One by one, the group took turns descending the slide—though Julie noticed that Rhonda held her vampire back behind the rest. She could only imagine what her friend was planning to do in that oddly mirrored room. And it made her wish it was *she* who was holding *Skeleton Guy* back. Even if she couldn't see his face. It didn't matter. In that moment she knew that Rhonda was right—seeing what he looked like wasn't important. Here, now, in a room surrounded by a hundred mirrors, it would make it even better.

Wow, you're perverse. This dress was having a seriously weird effect on her.

But she didn't really have time to contemplate it— she positioned herself carefully on the slide before letting go of the sides. Then she landed in a heap at the bottom, thankful she hadn't heard the dress rip anywhere. The base of the slide was cushioned, but as before, the air was pitch black. She could only hear the voices of the people in her group, couldn't see them, and she began to grope her way toward them.

Then a light suddenly shone before her—and it spotlighted a man with a hatchet buried in his bloody head. "Can you help me?" he asked her. Standing only a few feet away, he moved quickly closer. Then he drew a much larger ax from behind his back. "Or maybe you'd like one, too!"

Julie screamed and ran into the blackness. Bumping hard into a wall, she turned and ran in the opposite direction. She couldn't see a thing, but continued running anyway.

Footsteps sounded behind her, coming up quick. Oh God—the ax man was in hot pursuit! She had to get away! She had to find a way out! She had to get the hell out of this house before she lost her mind!

When two hands firmly grasped her waist, stopping her progress, her heart flew to her throat and she shut her eyes tight as if to block out the fear. "Pleeeease," she squeaked. *Please don't hurt me. Please don't kill me.* But all she could get out was that one word. Please.

As the hands propelled her body ahead through an open doorway, her eyes flew open. The thinnest hint of light seeped through a blackened window to shed a deadly pall on the room. She heard the door slam and realized she was no longer in the maniac's grasp—but when she started to move, the hands came back, gripping both her wrists tight. Her throat constricted and her chest grew taut with fear. The world seemed to spin. She closed her eyes again, trying to think, trying to breathe. Then felt herself being pushed back roughly against a wall.

She drew in her breath as the invisible heat of a body pressed against hers. Then a mouth, strong and hard, moist, came down against her lips.

She opened her eyes, frantic to see something, any-thing, frantic to make sense of what was happening. Then she made out the glow of white, almost gleaming against the black fabric of her dress. And she gasped at the realization that it was Skeleton Guy, becoming acutely aware that her body was melting with pleasure beneath his.

She was no longer afraid of the kiss, but hungrier for it than she'd ever been for a kiss in her life. She let her eyes fall closed again, then opened her mouth slightly to let his tongue enter. How deeply he kissed her, his tongue probing the insides of her mouth.

Her body grew rigid beneath his, her wrists still held firmly in his grasp. Her breasts strained against the snug dress and the spot between her legs went hot with desire. As she moved her mouth hard against his, her breath became rough, labored. She wanted more of the kissing and touching, more of *him*.

Then his still bone-clad hands found her neck, caressing her skin before his fingers fanned out through her hair. And when he reached the end of her shoulder-length locks, he stopped and pulled back, suddenly gazing upon her with widened eyes.

And said, "You're not Rachel!"

Chapter Four

———∿∿———

JULIE PULLED IN her breath and tried to calm the beating of her heart as mortification descended. He thought she was someone else! He thought she was Lady Godiva. How utterly humiliating. And infuriating on top of it.

"No, I'm not Rachel!" she said, angrily smoothing her dress in the darkness. "I'm Julie!"

"Julie?" he asked, perplexed. Then, "Witchiepoo?"

"Yes, Witchiepoo," she confirmed, exasperated.

As her eyes adjusted to the darkness, she watched the glowing bones of his fingers move back through his dark hair. "Geez," he said. "That dress must be tighter than I realized. I just saw the shape from behind and thought…"

"Hey, the dress might be a little snug, but I'd never wear anything as tacky as that Lady Godiva get-up."

"Call it tacky if you want, but it's pretty damn sexy if you ask me. Then again," he said, his voice softening as he peered down at her cleavage, "so is this."

She swallowed in dismay—because it sounded like

something Patrick would say and she wished she could ignore that. And she wished she could forget how angry she was at Skeleton Guy's mistake, and how stupid she felt for kissing him back. She wished she could just pull him down and kiss him again, stay in that room and kiss him forever. She wished none of the confusion mattered.

"Where's your hat?" he asked. "I'd have known it was you if you'd been wearing it."

Julie reached up to find nothing there—she hadn't realized it was gone. "I must've lost it somewhere. Maybe back in that horrible shaking room."

She saw his smile through the dim lighting. "I *liked* the shaking room."

"Oh?" she asked uncertainly.

"It did interesting things to that dress of yours."

"It did?"

Skeleton Guy laughed lightly. "As my grandpa used to say, it must be jelly 'cause jam don't shake like that."

The heat of fresh embarrassment bloomed on her cheeks.

"Seriously," he added, "you and that dress make a great combination."

She found herself squirming a little, uncomfortable at the new reality of being alone with him and his racy comments. "Basic black always looks good," she told him, as if to push away the compliment. "It's slimming and it flatters almost any figure. Plus it never goes out of style." God, what on earth was she babbling about? She sounded like Rhonda giving one of her documentary explanations.

"Black," he said in a raspy whisper. "It's so soothing and mysterious."

And she smiled despite herself. "Morticia Addams," she said, to let him know she understood the quote.

"On second thought, though," he added, "perhaps a cross between Morticia…and Ginger."

She lowered her chin slightly. "How did we get from the Addams Family to Gilligan's Island?"

"Before Ginger became a castaway she was voted 'Miss Hour Glass'. She had all the sand in all the right places." He smiled, then leaned closer, his voice becoming a low, sexy growl. "So do you."

She pulled in her breath, wishing she didn't need the emotion behind the sex. Wishing she didn't need the love, the human connection that came from the heart and the mind, not just the body. But she *did* need that. Or she at least needed the guy to know who he was kissing. Every ounce of tension from before had suddenly returned to the conversation. It seemed like a good time to change the subject.

"Yes, well, we'd better get out of here."

Skeleton Guy shrugged. "Guess you're right."

"You don't want to keep your girlfriend waiting, after all," she felt compelled to add.

"She's hardly my girlfriend," he replied, reaching for the doorknob. "I just met her tonight."

"Well, she's definitely a girl and you were definitely getting friendly with her."

Skeleton Guy stopped and turned back to face her. And he was smiling again. An incorrigible smile. "Are you jealous, Witchiepoo?"

Julie blinked. "Of course not."

"Because you had your chance, you know. But I got the idea you wanted nothing to do with me."

"Well, that was because…" She knew she'd given him a damn good reason back at the party, but standing so close to him in the dark just moments after such a passionate and intoxicating kiss, her mind went blank.

"Because of your homebody boyfriend," he said glumly. "I almost forgot."

"Who?" she said before she could catch herself.

"Huh?"

"Nothing," she said. "I was just…clearing my throat." She proceeded to clear her throat, attempting to make a 'who'ish noise that came out sounding as ridiculous as her explanation.

The doubtful glance he cast her in the dark room said he was wondering if anyone actually cleared their throat that way, and probably also wondering why she'd kissed him like that if she was so in love with someone else.

It came as a relief when he focused his attention back on the door, reaching to turn the knob. But it didn't budge. Skeleton Guy turned the old knob several times to no avail. "Damn thing's stuck," he muttered.

"Well, get it open," she said. "And fast."

He jiggled the doorknob again and soon appeared to

be wrestling with it, the only sound that of a rusted lock clicking uselessly.

"Damn," he groused.

Then Julie said, "Wait. Listen."

And he stilled the movement of his hand long enough for them both to hear it. Silence. Everywhere.

"There's nobody in the house anymore," she realized out loud, her voice edged with panic. She feared her heart would burst right through her chest.

"Stay calm," he instructed. "Don't crack up on me like you did back with that chainsaw. They've got to be out there somewhere. They wouldn't leave without us."

"You're right," she agreed. "Of course they wouldn't. What am I thinking?"

Then the silence gave way to a muffled noise somewhere nearby, yet seemingly far away, and they squinted at each other in the darkness. "Is that what I think it is?" he asked.

And she nodded. The sound of car engines starting.

"Jesus," he said. "I can't believe they're leaving us."

"Shhh," she said, listening again.

A mix of muted noises met their ears. The vague blur of a car radio. And a barrage of muffled voices.

One of the voices belonged to Rhonda. "Julie?" she called. "Julie?" She thought she could make out another deeper voice yelling her name as well and guessed it might be Rhonda's vampire.

"Scott?" another muted female voice yelled. "Scott, where are you?"

Julie looked up at Skeleton Guy. "Was that your nude girlfriend?"

"How many times do I have to tell you? She's not my girlfriend."

"Well, you thought you were kissing her."

"A kiss does not a girlfriend make."

"That's for sure," she muttered.

"And besides," he said, "maybe deep down I sort of knew…"

"What?"

He glanced at her sideways. "Nothing."

"Nothing?"

Lady Godiva's muffled voice came again and Julie's gaze met Scott's just briefly before they unspeakingly realized they were wasting time and both dashed toward the blackened window.

"Hey, we're in here!" Scott yelled.

"Help!" she called. "Help us! We're trapped!"

Standing side by side, they both beat on the window. Scott gripped at its edges, trying to find a way to open it up. And Julie kept yelling, certain someone would hear. But the faint voices continued calling their names outside, unable to detect their cries.

She listened as Rhonda's shouts grew more desperate.

Then she heard someone outside say, "Calm down. They're searching the house."

"They're searching the house," she repeated frantically to her companion. "They're searching the house."

So the two of them rushed back toward the door and

began to beat on it and yell.

"Hey, get us out of here!" Julie screamed.

"Up here!" Scott yelled. "We're up here!"

"Up?" she asked. "What do you mean *up*?"

"I'm pretty sure we're on the second floor," he said.

"How could you tell with all those stairs and slides?" And given that the room's window had been blackened, that hadn't given her any sense of orientation, either.

"I don't know," he said. "Good sense of direction, I guess."

"Then keep yelling it to them," she said, deciding she believed him as she turned back to the door. "We're on the second floor!" she bellowed.

"Upstairs!" he joined in. "Second floor!"

After another minute of making noise, though, they finally stopped. Nothing in the house seemed to be moving.

"They're not looking anymore," she finally whispered. And she sank to her knees in despair.

Scott lingered above her for a moment, then dropped down on his knees, too, facing her. They looked forlornly into each other's eyes. Part of her wanted to kiss him. And part of her wanted to rip him apart for dragging her into that room in the first place.

But they both stayed quiet and finally discerned more of the barely audible voices from below. She could only catch bits and pieces of the conversation beneath the music from the car radio.

"… must have taken a ride back with somebody

else…"

"Julie wouldn't do that," she heard Rhonda say. "Not without letting me know."

"… only explanation…go back to the party…they'll be there…probably don't even know we're worried."

Then Julie heard the car doors closing, their last chance for rescue dying with each slam.

The two of them stayed silent, each wallowing in private gloom. The last few cars could be heard pulling slowly away into the distance, the music growing fainter until eventually no sound remained at all.

Finally Scott spoke. "Guess you can't get us out of this with a twitch of your nose?"

Julie peeked up at him with disbelieving eyes, but she refused to respond. This was no time for witch humor.

"So," he began when she didn't answer, "you're just like poor Aunt Clara on Bewitched."

"What?" she finally whispered.

"Lost your powers."

She just grimaced.

And he swallowed visibly. "Sorry," he said. "Just trying to make the best of a bad situation."

"What are we gonna do?" she asked.

"Well," he began, "I guess the workers will be back tomorrow night. It'll be Halloween."

But his words only made her shudder in the surrounding darkness. "Tomorrow night! You're suggesting we wait here for twenty-four hours?"

He shrugged. "Got any better ideas, Witchiepoo?"

"My name's Julie," she reminded him.

"Yeah, well, it's hard to get used to that after calling you Witchiepoo all night."

"Speaking of 'all night', I'm not about to just sit here. Can't you try to break down that door?" She paused, trying not to let the darkened corners of the room lure her eyes. "I really can't bear the thought of sitting in this dark, creepy house all night. I don't like haunted houses."

"I noticed."

"And I'm feeling claustrophobic," she confessed.

He pursed his skeleton lips, clearly thinking. "All right," he said. "Move out of the way and I'll try to get us out of here."

Julie rose to her feet and backed away from the door, then watched as he stepped back and ran toward it—only to bash his shoulder into an unbudging slab of wood.

"Damn," he said, "this thing's like a concrete wall."

But when he ran at the door a second time, she heard the lock rattle at the impact; perhaps it was starting to give.

"Try again," she instructed him anxiously.

He was bent over, hands on his knees, trying to catch his breath. "Would you mind if I took half a second to regain my strength?"

"Sorry," she mumbled. "I just want out of here."

He sighed, seeming annoyed, but readied himself to take another lunge at the old wooden door—only to stop and glance up. "Hey," he said, "look." He pointed up above the door and Julie strained her eyes to see.

"I think there's an old transom window up there," he explained of the brown rectangle of paper that stretched across the top of the door. And then he leaped like a basketball player doing a layup, extending his arm to poke at the paper with his hand. The paper gave way, falling through the other side of the missing window, and Julie cheered his success.

"Come on," Scott said, looking back at her.

He held out his bone-covered hand and she moved shyly forward and took it in hers.

"I'll need to boost you up and through the window," he went on.

Okay, she hadn't thought ahead to that part, even though it was obvious. But there was no other choice, so she just nodded.

"Now," he said, still holding her hand, "put one foot on my right knee."

So she carefully lifted her foot, still worried about ripping the tight dress, then planted her left pump on the top of Scott's thigh.

"Ow!" he said. "Get off me, Witchiepoo."

And she stepped back down, confused.

"Those heels have got to go," he told her, bending toward her feet. She lifted them, one at a time, and he deftly removed the shoes, tossing them easily up and out through the transom. They landed with two distinctive clunks on the other side as she grimaced at having to stand in her bare feet on the gritty old floor.

"Now," Scott said, "let's try this again."

She took a deep breath and planted one foot firmly on his knee. As she gripped his leg with her toes, she couldn't ignore the solid warmth beneath her sole that moved briskly up her calf and thigh, and then spread through her whole body.

"Sit on my shoulder," he instructed, "then I'll raise you up to the window."

Julie positioned herself as instructed, grabbing on to his other shoulder so she wouldn't fall. And he slowly rose to a complete upright position and moved to the door with her body perched above him.

Her heart pounded mercilessly when his hands melted into her hips to lift her to the window. And, like back at the party, she found herself trying to envision the male hands beneath the fabric, what they would look like, feel like, touching her. She bit her lip, wanting to concentrate on the task at hand, but far more caught up in the sensation of being in his grasp.

Ready to attempt an exit, she stuck her head through the window. But as she began to maneuver her shoulders into the narrow rectangle, she unexpectedly caught her chest on the metal edge that lined the bottom of the opening. "Ouch," she squeaked, instinctively jerking away and letting her weight fall back on Scott.

He lost his balance for a moment, swaying, and she reached for the transom's edge as he tottered uncertainly beneath her. When he spoke his voice came out muffled.

"Witchiepoo, you're smothering me."

Then he gave a huge shove, propelling her through the window up to her waist, so that half her body was inside the room, the other half out.

She balanced precariously in the window for a moment, feeling the full mortification of where her butt had obviously just been—just before Scott's fabric-covered hands closed on her ankles, giving her another unexpected push.

Groping at the walls on either side of the door, she got hold of an old wall lamp and managed to lower herself to the floor in the hallway with only a light thud. And as she scampered to retrieve her shoes, hurriedly sliding her feet back into them in an effort to salvage any remaining remnants of composure, Scott glided gracefully through the window above her with the agility of a cat.

"You all right?" he asked, lowering himself easily to the floor.

"Yes," she replied. Then, "Um, sorry about smothering you."

He grinned. "Under other circumstances, it would have made me a very happy man."

And despite herself, she couldn't stop the rise of heat to her face. Dress comments were one thing, and even shaking room talk could be tolerated, but this was a step too far. She drew her eyes from his, trying to hide her embarrassment, but it didn't work.

"Sorry, Witchiepoo," he said, his tone softening. "That just popped out. I didn't mean to…"

"What? Didn't mean to what?"

"Nothing," he replied, suddenly averting his eyes. But he still spoke more gently than usual. "Come on, let's get out of here."

The walk was treacherous without the aid of lights, but it was better than being stuck in that room. And it gave her something else to focus on besides the tense moments she'd experienced with him, seemingly one after another, since getting trapped together.

"I feel like we're walking in circles," she told him, half to break the tension of her own thoughts and half because it was true.

"Trust me," he whispered over his shoulder. And she only wished it were that easy.

"I think we missed the stairway back there," she offered.

"And I think you should trust me," he simply replied.

She didn't respond, but only sighed to herself and continued to follow him. At least it seemed like some sort of progress. And maybe he knew exactly where he was going. He'd said he had a good sense of direction, after all.

She gasped when her eyes fell on a bloody corpse in the corner of a room—but then she remembered that they were in a haunted house and it wasn't real. And when they passed through the chainsaw room again, she remembered the very real terror she'd felt there as well. Seemed that Scott remembered it, too.

"Hey," he said, stopping to glance back at her, his eyes shining like tiny crystals in the darkness, "why'd you freak out in here before?"

She took a deep breath. "It's stupid," she said, gently pushing him forward with one hand in hopes of moving away from all the imaginary blood and death.

"I don't doubt that," he told her matter-of-factly, "but tell me anyway."

She didn't relish the idea of sharing the truth with him, but knew she was poor at lying. Well, except about fake boyfriends. Still, she didn't feel quick-witted enough at the moment to come up with anything but honesty.

"As soon as I saw that guy," she began, shoving Scott farther up the hall, "I got this horrible idea. I thought— what if some psycho signed up to work in the haunted house and snuck in a real chainsaw and started carving people up?"

Scott stayed silent and continued inching his way forward in the dark. She wished she could see his expression.

"Stupid, huh?" she asked.

"Nothing like that has ever occurred to me before," he confessed. "So I'll probably never be able to walk through a haunted house again, thank you very much."

"Sorry," she murmured. And, for some reason suffering the need to say more, she sighed and muttered yet another painful truth about herself to a man she hardly knew. "That's just how I am."

"*What's* just how you are?"

"I...get a little irrational," she explained. "I get scared."

"Why?"

"It's just my nature. I like things to be dependable. Safe. So little is, you know." She pulled in her breath then, sorry to have tossed in that last little bit of fearful honesty.

He stopped and looked back at her. Then he spoke slowly. "I guess I can understand what you mean. The world isn't always pretty."

"Exactly," she said. "So I try to concentrate on the parts that are. That's why I don't like haunted houses. I figure, why dredge up fear in a world where there's already plenty to be afraid of?"

Scott raised one glowing finger in the air. "But I think that's just it," he said. "I think people go to haunted houses to *face* their fears."

"Hmm," she said, realizing that... "I guess actually that's part of why *I* agreed to come here, now that I think about it." She left out that the other part was a misguided attempt to win him away from Lady Godiva.

"That's good," he told her. "Sort of takes a negative and turns it positive, you know?"

Julie stayed silent, following behind, suddenly feeling a small connection between them. She hadn't expected him to understand her irrational fears. And she certainly hadn't expected him to enlighten her on anything, but he kind of had.

"I wish we could find that room with the strobe

lighting," he said then.

"Why?" she asked.

"I've always wondered what it would be like to have sex under a strobe light."

She stopped short, his hand still in hers, and he jerked to a halt in front of her. "Excuse me," she said. "Are you suggesting that you think I would have sex with you beneath a strobe light? Beneath *any* light?"

"You kissed me pretty hot and heavy in that dark room," he observed with an arrogant grin.

Pulling in her breath as she fumed, she yanked her hand away from his. Every time she started to believe he was human, he did something to change her mind.

Despite her reaction, though, he still smiled at her in the darkness. "You don't like me very much, do you, Witchiepoo?"

She sighed and kept it simple. "Well, certainly not enough for that. I don't even know you."

"But I don't think you *want* to know me, do you? After all, if you want to have sex underneath a strobe light, you've got that boyfriend to do it with, right?"

Oops, she sort of kept forgetting about him. So she kept that simple, too. "Excuse me, but I'll thank you to leave my sex life out of this." *As if I have one.*

"I bet Mr. Stay-At-Home wouldn't want to do anything that wild, though, would he?" Scott asked. "I bet he's a real under-the-covers, missionary position kind of guy."

Unable to think of an answer, she didn't give one.

But she wished Scott would quit trying to imagine her sex life with Mr. Stay-At-Home. And she wished Mr. Stay-At-Home actually existed. She thought he might have been a pretty nice guy.

"I know you liked kissing me, Witchiepoo," Scott said, his voice brimming with arrogant confidence. "Or did you even know who you were kissing in the dark?"

"I knew," she said casually. Then in explanation, "Your bones glow."

"So you're not as repelled by me as you like to pretend."

She tried to sound a bit smug. "Who ever said I was repelled? I merely said I was unavailable."

"Your words may have said 'unavailable'," he told her, "but your actions said something else."

"What's that supposed to mean?" she snipped, tensing.

"I'd just like to know what that kiss was all about," he said over his shoulder with a too-confident shrug and an infuriating little grin.

"Nothing." She sounded even more snappish now, fearing the truth might come out, that he might actually persuade her to admit her attraction to him. "That kiss was about nothing."

"Aren't you at least tempted, Witchiepoo?" he asked. "To find that room and flip on that strobe light and let me—"

"Shut up," she told him.

And he went amazingly quiet at her command. "I

know you think I'm a really crude guy," he finally said, "but I'm just playing with you. Just joking around. I thought I was being funny, but obviously I wasn't. I apologize."

Julie didn't respond, caught off guard, but when he reached for her hand again, she let it close around hers. Despite everything, his touch made her feel safer, less afraid of what she couldn't see in the dark. And while some of the things he'd said had embarrassed her, she was equally as embarrassed by her own desire for him, a desire she was trying desperately to hide. She bit her lip in the darkness, wondering why she had to be so frightened.

She walked behind him again, thinking of Patrick. Patrick would have loved the idea about the strobe light. And like every wild impulse of Patrick's that had included her, she would have been repulsed.

Up until this moment, she'd always thought it was her, that she was prudish. That had been Patrick's word for her—prude. It had never occurred to her that wild suggestions from someone else could have a different, even opposite effect on her. But hearing such things from Scott had felt strangely different. Even without knowing him. Even without being able to see him, his face. Hearing such things from Scott felt…almost tempting.

If, that is, she hadn't been lying to him so much. And if he hadn't mistaken her for another woman in the dark. And if she hadn't been so afraid to let herself…feel anything for a man.

Something in her chest deflated.

Since when are you afraid of your own feelings?

Since now.

Her relationship with Patrick, especially the ending, had been devastating. And the true impact of that had just hit her freshly in the darkness. No wonder she hadn't wanted to come to this party, or to meet guys. She wasn't *ready* to trust a man again. Not *any* man. But especially not a man with a suggestive sense of humor who seemed completely ready to seduce the nearest available girl.

Julie followed Scott carefully down a steep flight of stairs. She rested her hands on his shoulders for balance to avoid touching walls that might have God-only-knew-what on them. And she wished desperately that those shoulders didn't feel so broad and strong beneath her hands.

Descending the steps in her heels gave her the sensation of toppling forward, causing her to grip his shoulders even more firmly through the Skeleton costume. "Witchiepoo," she heard him say below her, "don't put so much weight on my—"

And then they fell. Scott's legs folded beneath him and he bumped down the steps on his rear as Julie tumbled forward on him, her arms closing around his neck as she followed his rough descent. She knew she was probably strangling him as they went down, but she couldn't let go. When they landed with a hard thud at the base of the stairs, her upper body smashed tightly into his back, her legs curling up beneath her.

Her entire body ached, but at the same time, she barely noticed. She couldn't believe that even in this bizarre situation, the only thing she could think about was being pressed up against him so firmly.

"You okay?" she asked timidly.

"Yeah. You?"

"I think so."

He gingerly unwrapped her arms from around his neck. "Witchiepoo?" he said quietly.

"Yes?"

"Try not to kill me before we get out of here, okay?"

"Okay," she whispered.

Then she looked up. They had landed right before the front door of the old house! "Scott," she said, pointing over his shoulder, "I think we made it."

In response, he got to his feet and stepped to the entrance, Julie standing up next to him. He turned the lock, then opened the door with a loud squeak—and together they looked out on the moonlit darkness as a soft breeze wafted over them. Fields of broken down cornstalks on either side of the house were silhouetted in the dim, eerie light. And beyond, in all directions, the edges of billowy tree lines seemed to glow beneath the moon. Not a light could be seen.

"Sorry to let you down, Witchiepoo," Scott said, "but I don't think we've made it quite yet."

Chapter Five

———◆◆◆———

J ULIE CLUTCHED SCOTT'S hand as he led the way, a gentle autumn breeze blowing around them, stirring fallen leaves and pulling still more from tree limbs.

The heels of her shoes dug into the soft earth between the rows of old corn, making it difficult to walk, but Scott thought following the cornfields might provide a shorter route to the main road than traversing the twisting gravel drive that had brought them there. Knowing he had a good sense of direction, Julie had agreed to let him choose their route. He'd gotten them out of the house, after all.

"Best TV dog?" Scott asked her.

Julie pondered the question. "I guess I'd have to go with Tramp on *My Three Sons.*"

"Wimp answer," he replied.

"What? Tramp was a perfectly nice dog."

"Right. Who belonged to a perfectly nice family on a perfectly nice show. Too easy. No guts."

"Sorry," she said. "I didn't know answering a question about TV dogs required guts. What's *your* answer?"

"Toss-up," he replied. "Buck on *Married With Children*—now there's a real dog, a dog with personality, a dog with a life, a dog who has the sense to enjoy a scantily-clad babe. So I'd pick either him or Simone on *The Partridge Family*."

"Simone on *The Partridge Family*?" she asked. "I don't even recall such a dog."

He shook his head skeptically. "You must have been too busy mooning over Keith. Simone wins on the simple principal of having a great dog name."

"How about Dino?" Julie suggested.

And Scott stopped briefly to glance over his shoulder with a you've-got-to-be-kidding look before turning back to trudge through the dirt. "Dino was not a dog," he pointed out, his voice full of condescension.

"But they *called* him a dog."

"He looks far too much like Barney to get a vote from me."

"Barney…Rubble?" She was confused.

"No, not Barney Rubble. Barney the dinosaur."

"Oh," she said, "so you hate all lovable dinosaurs."

"Just the purple ones," he replied.

"Okay, I've got one. Best superhero. I vote for Wonder Woman."

"How typical of you."

She let out a *harrumph* behind him.

"Really," he said, "she was built, true, but if you're gonna go the feminist route on me, at least be original. Batgirl. Isis. Somebody like that."

Julie smirked. "All right, then," she said, "*your* vote for best superhero?"

He deliberated for a moment before he thoughtfully replied, "Hong Kong Phooey."

She released a sigh of annoyance. "Hong Kong Phooey was not a superhero. He was a dog who did karate."

"He also did superhero stuff like solving crimes and catching bad guys."

"Well, so did Scooby Doo and Speed Buggy and half a million others, but that doesn't put them in the category of superhero."

"He was a superhero," Scott insisted quietly.

"The dog learned karate from a correspondence course," Julie pointed out. "He changed into his costume in a filing cabinet. He was *not*, I repeat *not*, a superhero."

"Was too."

"Did he belong to the League of Justice?"

Scott hesitated, then quietly admitted the truth. "No."

"There," she snapped. "No League of Justice membership, no superhero."

"Tell me something, Witchiepoo," he said.

"What would you like to know?" She continued walking behind him, waiting for more stunning repartee on the differentiation between superheroes and non-superheroes.

"Why'd you lie to me?" he asked her instead.

Uh-oh. Had he figured her out? That she didn't really have a stay-at-home boyfriend? Or any boyfriend? Her stomach churned with all the possible ramifications. "Lie?" she said. "About what?"

"Why'd you tell me you were a model?"

A heavy sigh escaped her. This seemed almost worse than the boyfriend issue. How stupid she felt all over again. And how much more she'd rather discuss... "Best TV apartment?"

Scott stopped and turned to chide her with his eyes.

"I vote for *The Monkees*," she said quickly. "They had that really cool spiral staircase."

Scott sighed and gave in. "Okay, I'll say *Three's Company* because it gave you the idea that it was on the beach. As well as in walking distance of the Regal Beagle. But really," he said softly, "why'd you lie to me?"

She swallowed nervously. "I thought we covered that already."

"Not enough. It was loud at the party, hard to talk, so I let you off easy. But we've got plenty of time now, and plenty of quiet, so why don't you explain it to me in a little more detail."

She stayed quiet for a moment, thinking. And he didn't press her to start, but waited patiently, still forging their path through the old rows of corn.

"It was actually Rhonda's idea," she began.

"The kinky devil?"

"Yes." She took a deep breath. "She thinks I don't get out enough, thinks I don't have very much adventure in my life, I guess. She suggested, since no one would know me at the party, that I...kind of experiment with a new identity. I don't know why I did it. It just popped out. Maybe I wanted to see if I could make somebody believe something like that about me."

"I believed it."

"You didn't see the antique dealer lurking within?"

"Nope," he said. "Any woman who can fill out that dress the way you do gets my vote to be a model any day."

"That's another thing," she went on. "This dress. It belongs to Rhonda. She made me go to the party. She made me wear it. I'm usually much more conservative. This dress isn't me."

"I beg to differ," he said.

"What?"

"That dress most certainly *is* you."

"How would you know?"

"You walk into a room in it and knock every man out. You carry yourself in it like a movie star. Or a model. Maybe that's why I believed it. You move great in that dress, trust me. If the dress wasn't you, you'd cower in it, or be stiff as a board. But you're not. You're totally graceful in it."

"I am?" She didn't feel very graceful plodding through the field, her heels digging into the dirt with each step, but his words made her feel strangely special.

"Why are you so afraid of it?" he asked her.

"So afraid of what?"

"So afraid of how good you look in that dress. It's

not a crime. Or a sin. It's how God made you."

"Let's not bring God into this," she said, trying to head him off at the pass.

"Why not? Are you an atheist or something?"

"No. And I'm not so sure He's crazy about this dress."

"I disagree completely," Scott said. "Why would He have given you those curves if He'd meant them to be hidden?"

"Look," she said, "I think this takes us back to that whole Garden of Eden scene, and no matter how much time we may have on our hands, I'm just not sure I want to get into that with you."

"Why not?" He looked over his shoulder; raised his eyebrows. "Afraid I'll win?" Then he turned back ahead.

"Win what?"

"The argument we're about to have."

"We're not about to have an argument, Scott, because we're not discussing it."

"Yes we are, and I'm going to point out to you that despite all that serpent business, men and women have spent thousands of years evolving and I think we're finally on our way back to how things started, how things are supposed to be. Where you're not supposed to feel any shame over your beauty."

"It's not a matter of beauty," she protested. "It's a matter of my body. And my personal preference is to keep it under wraps. A few fig leaves don't cut it for me."

"It's a matter of a *beautiful* body," he corrected her,

"and *my* personal preference is to see it. For you to *want* me to see it."

He halted and turned so abruptly that Julie stopped short and tripped over a root. And she was almost thankful when her body tumbled clumsily into his because it kept her from having to deal with the last words he'd said. It also kept her from being able to verify the look of desire she thought she'd seen burning in his eyes.

He tried to catch her as she fell, but only succeeded in being knocked backwards on the ground—and she landed sprawled across his glowing legs, her cheek pressed solidly against one hard thigh. She drew in her breath as a nervous heat whisked down through her body—because she wanted to kiss him there, on his warm, muscular leg. She quickly rose up off him into a kneeling position.

"There you go again," he said, sitting up in the dirt. "Trying to kill me."

"Sorry," she said. "I guess I'm getting tired."

"Past your bedtime?"

"You could say that."

"I guess Home Boy is missing you terribly."

She wished he'd quit bringing her imaginary boyfriend into the conversation. "Probably," she said shortly.

That was when she followed Scott's eyes and realized they were planted squarely on her cleavage again. He seemed very attracted to it. Then again, the dress asked for that, she supposed. Invited it.

In one sense, his intense gaze there set off tiny sparks of excitement inside her. But in another way, it made her feel as if she were on display, like she'd always felt with Patrick. The memory made her need to change things somehow and the onset of nerves caused her to push to her feet.

"Let's get going," she said. "I'd like to find a house—that's occupied and not haunted—before morning." She trudged ahead in the dirt, forcing him to catch up.

"Don't hit me if I tell you something," he said, falling into step behind her.

"What?" she asked, dreading his reply.

"You're going to think this is totally lewd, rude, and crude, but I just can't help myself. You have beautiful breasts."

A rush of blood encased Julie from head to toe. She couldn't believe him! After all this, what on earth made him think it was okay to say such a thing? And as for the inexplicable and undeniably tingly sensation coursing through her veins…well, she just tried to ignore that and commanded herself to play it cool. So she came back with, "How would you know? You've never seen them."

"I can see enough," he said.

"Only because of the dress," she shot back, still plodding ahead. "No wonder you think it's so 'me'."

"Even without the dress," he said. But then stopped, quietly chuckling at his own faux pas before he continued. "What I mean is that it wouldn't matter what you were wearing. I'd still be able to tell."

"X-Ray vision? Where's the blue suit and red cape?"

"I don't need to be Superman—even Jimmy Olsen would be able to see it. It's a guy thing," he said. "We can tell."

She flashed a brief glance at him over her shoulder, eyebrows raised. "Oh? How?"

"It's an instinct sort of thing," he explained as they walked. "Something innate. A sixth sense, if you will."

"So your extra-sensory perception has told you that I have nice boobs."

"Beautiful," he corrected her. "And it didn't hurt to press up against them when we kissed either."

Julie was dumbfounded. Grounded by the memory of their kiss, of their bodies pressing so warmly together. And strangely infatuated with a form of flattery that normally would have offended her. Even if it somehow hadn't as much as usual, whether or not she'd tried to feel that way.

Still, she didn't quite know how to just accept it. She *wasn't* a model, after all, not someone used to thinking of her body as something for public consumption. She was Julie the insecure antique dealer, not quite sure how to be anything *but* insecure. Some things were just in-grained.

"Look," she said, turning to face him and deciding to put an end to his infatuation with that part of her body, "it's the bra."

"*What?*" he asked, confused.

"It's the bra I'm wearing. It pushes them up. It

squeezes them together. I hate to squash your fantasies and tell you all my secrets, but there it is. The enigma surrounding my cleavage is out."

"You still have to have something to put in it," he said simply.

"Huh?"

"You heard me," he said. Then, "Geez, try to give somebody a compliment and get attacked with tales of the killer bra."

Now she felt suddenly stupid, but defended herself anyway. "Well, it was a rather unusual compliment to get from someone I just met."

"Yeah, well, sorry," he said, sounding annoyed, "but we happen to be in a pretty unusual predicament. I said what I thought, what I felt like saying. I keep forgetting."

"Forgetting what?"

"That you don't like honesty."

Julie gasped—she couldn't believe his way of twisting her reactions. "Honesty is great," she told him. "When appropriate."

"Under the circumstances, I think it's *very* appropriate," he argued.

"Wait. Let me get this straight," she said, stopping and turning to hold up her hands before plodding onward. "You think the things you've been saying to me are perfectly appropriate to say to someone you've just met?"

"To someone I've just met who I already feel comfortable with," he corrected her. "Who I'm obviously going to be spending several more hours with tonight. Who I've already made out with for a few minutes. Who I'm attracted to. And who I think is also attracted to me."

She stopped again—this time turning fully to face him, hands planted firmly on her hips.

"I know, I know," he said, "your heart belongs to Home Boy."

"Yes."

"And you expect me to believe that it's not possible for you to be attracted to me in spite of that. That your hormones only work for him. That you weren't into that really long kiss we shared. Well, if that's the way you want to play it, Witchiepoo, okay. Who am I to come along and mess up your happy little engagement?"

"As if you could," she spewed.

"Don't worry," he said. "I'm not planning on trying."

And despite her irritation, she was a little hurt by his words—but she kept her voice stern. "Oh, is that so?"

"Look, it's obvious to me by now that you're a very nice woman. A little too demure for my taste, but that's your prerogative. At any rate, I can see that even if you didn't have Mr. Stay-At-Home to keep you warm at night that you wouldn't be out looking for fun, that you'd want something a lot safer than that, probably something a lot more secure."

"So?" she said.

"So that wouldn't be me."

"Hmm," she said, wanting to know what that meant. And why it bothered her so much. "And just when I was beginning to think you might be a decent guy after all."

"I am," he claimed. "But I'm just not looking for anything…you know, serious."

How typical. And something about it made her turn back around and resume trudging forward. "How old are you?" she asked.

"Thirty-two. Why?"

"One of those little boys who just can't stand to grow up and settle down?"

"It's been tried," he said.

"What do you mean?"

"I tried to settle down once and it didn't work out. End of discussion."

"Please don't address me as if I'm Edith Bunker," she said dryly. "And as you like to point out, we have all night here, so explain yourself."

He shifted his weight from one hiking boot to the other in the cornfield. "Let's just say I don't necessarily believe in true love, happy endings, all that jazz."

"What do you believe in then?"

"Good fun, good laughs, good sex."

"Hence your preoccupation with my dress."

"Precisely," he concurred.

"So what happened?" she asked, letting her voice soften. "To make you ditch the happy ending stuff?"

"I didn't get one."

"Come on," she said. "Would you quit being so

cryptic? I told you about my bra, and I even explained to you why I lied about being a model. This is the first thing I've asked you. Now play fair."

Scott stayed silent for a minute, still walking behind her—until he finally told her, "I was married."

Julie drew to a quick halt and he bumped into her, jostling them both.

"Would you quit that?" he said.

"You were married?" she shot over her shoulder. He definitely didn't seem like the marrying kind.

He just sighed and pointed ahead into the darkness of the cornfield before them. "Walk," he instructed her, "and I'll talk."

She turned back around, moving forward again.

"The long and the short of it," he began, "is that you can think you know someone better than you know yourself, and then one day you can wake up and find out you never really knew them at all."

"What happened?"

He hesitated, then said, "Some other guy," obviously working to blot out the strain in his voice.

A sharp pang of compassion shot through her as she took that in, both touched and surprised. How human he sounded, despite how hard he tried not to. She almost regretted having asked him to talk about it.

"I'm sorry," she told him.

"He was a heart surgeon," he said, his voice back to normal. "Can you believe that? Talk about being impossible to compete with."

"Did you want to?" Julie asked. "I mean, after you found out. Did you want to get her back?" She recalled her own emotions when she'd first confirmed that Patrick was cheating on her. She'd wondered if anyone else had ever felt so confused.

"It's a complicated question," he replied. "At first you want things to work out somehow. You want to do whatever it takes the make the trouble go away, to make things go back to how they used to be. But we couldn't go back. Which really pissed her off."

"What do you mean?"

"Well, she decided she wanted things the way they used to be, too—but I just didn't feel the same anymore. I *couldn't* feel the same—couldn't figure out *how* to. The divorce was hell."

"How long were you married?"

"Six years. The divorce was final last July, but we'd been separated for a year before that. I'm over it. I mean, I hope she's happy. And I hope *I'm* happy."

"Are you?" Julie asked, biting her lip, glad he couldn't see the concern on her face.

"Yeah." His voice rang with conviction. Like maybe it was something he had just recently gotten back. "Yeah," he said again, "I really am."

"Even though you don't believe in happily ever after anymore."

"Maybe I still *believe* in it," he said. "Maybe I just think happily ever after doesn't always have to involve a companion. Maybe I think a person can be happy on his own."

Scott's words twisted Julie's stomach into knots. *She* didn't feel that way and she didn't want *him* to feel that way either. She'd believed in romance and true love and soulmates ever since she'd seen the movie *Cinderella* as a little girl. And she thought every woman had a Prince Charming waiting for her somewhere out there. Even after what had happened with Patrick, she wasn't ready to completely turn her back on love yet.

And still, if this was how Scott felt—well, it might not have anything to do with her but it was still hard not to take it personally somehow. After all, he'd pretty much said that even if she were free as a bird, he'd want nothing more from her than casual fun and sex.

"I guess you're right then," she told him.

"About what?"

"That you wouldn't be the guy for me."

He stayed quiet for a moment, then finally said, "I hope I didn't hurt your feelings, Julie." It was the first time he'd said her name.

And of course, she lied. "No—of course not."

"I still believe in relationships," he told her. "I still believe in caring about people. I just wouldn't be too crazy about committing my life to someone again."

She took a deep breath and tried to quell the churning in her stomach. She didn't want to feel rejected and hurt. And she didn't want to care about changing his mind. But despite herself, she did. He was way too young to give up on love. "Well," she finally said, "I don't think you should base your whole view of forever on one experience."

"Easy for you to say," he told her.

And she was tempted to tell him that it *wasn't* easy for her to say, not at all, and that she was bouncing back from a rotten, cheat-ridden relationship too—yet that she hadn't given up on the notion of commitment entirely.

Not in theory anyway. She'd been running from him all night, of course, which wasn't exactly a good sign in her recovery process.

But at least she hadn't turned against the whole idea of true love and happiness.

Only she couldn't tell him *any* of that because of her dumb imaginary boyfriend. So she decided it was probably a good idea to just take the conversation in a whole different direction.

"Look at the stars," she said, stopping to lean her head back to peer at the sky.

And Scott plowed into her and sent them both tumbling to the ground.

Instead of yelling at her this time, though, he merely followed her instruction and gazed upward from his new spot in the dirt. "Nice," he said about the stars.

And she thought out loud, saying, "This isn't so awful."

"Isn't it?" He drew his eyes back down, his gaze laced with amusement now, to meet hers. "I think we may kill each other before the night's over."

"Of course," she said, "you probably wish you were stuck out here with Lady Godiva. But then again, if that were the case, you'd have just stayed back at the haunted house with the strobe light, huh?"

His eyes released a thick heat that flowed out over her when she least expected it. "The truth is, I'd much rather be stuck out here with you, Witchiepoo."

And her heart fluttered in surprise—but she quickly looked away, afraid of encouraging him, afraid of encouraging *herself*, afraid of all the emotions bubbling in her heart.

THEY TROD SILENTLY through yet another cornfield, Scott's eyes on Julie's back. More precisely, on her hips. What a body—he could look at the curves in that dress forever.

He wondered how long it had been since they'd spoken. It had clearly been a mistake to tell her he'd rather be stuck out here with her instead of Lady Godiva since she hadn't uttered a word since. It had probably scared her. *Everything* scared her.

Of course, he knew he shouldn't have said some of those things to her earlier. He shouldn't have said *most* of those things. But time after time, he'd spoken without forethought, oblivious to the outcome. He'd been acting like a jerk and he knew it. He just couldn't seem to stop it.

He obviously shouldn't have taken his allergy pills

before the party. And he obviously shouldn't have started drinking rum punch, either. The combination had blurred his good sense for a while. Talk about losing his inhibitions…

But…maybe a part of him had wanted that. Maybe a part of him had just been having a little fun, trying to loosen up for a change. And the convenience of wearing a disguise had only added to it—that feeling that he was free to say whatever was on his mind without censoring himself.

He spent a lot of time being straight-laced and responsible and he'd come to the party tonight looking for…something. Freedom? His lost youth? He wasn't sure if making lewd remarks to a beautiful woman helped attain either of those things, but with the added influence of too many substances in his body at once, he'd found himself unable to shut up. He hadn't meant to upset Witchiepoo. Although he had to admit she was gorgeous when she was angry.

He didn't think he'd ever met such a strange and infuriating woman in his life. Everything about her screamed confusion. She shows up at a wild party only to claim she's the stay-at-home type. She pours herself into the hottest, tightest dress he's ever seen, then spends the whole night saying *how dare you* and playing Little Miss Prim and Proper. She tells him she models bikinis—lying no less—then gets all bent out of shape when he acts interested in her body. And, oh yeah, his favorite, she's madly in love, even engaged, to some guy without the sense to keep an eye on her, but she kisses him in the dark like she's been in exile for years.

Scott smiled, glad she couldn't see his face at the moment. That kiss had been incredible. He might have expected something like that from Rachel and her Lady Godiva suit—but not from Witchiepoo. He'd been totally shocked to find Miss How Dare You herself standing beneath him with her hungry eyes and pouting lips. Shocked not because it was her. He'd known good and well who he was kissing, but for some reason had felt the need to lie about it. What had shocked him was the energy behind the kiss. The heat, the desire. Maybe *that* was what had caused him to play dumb—utter shock at Witchiepoo's sensuous kiss.

How much in love could a woman be with a guy if she was kissing another man that way? He could allow for general passion, getting caught up in the moment, that sort of thing—that happened to people sometimes, even people with the best of intentions. But the way she'd kissed him had gone far beyond simple passion. It had been like electricity. Like fire. Everything hot. They had sizzled together in that darkened room. He wished they could sizzle some more.

Actually, he wished they could do more than just sizzle. Despite himself, something about the woman intrigued him. So she'd lied. And she was hard to get along with. Not to mention being ridiculously self-righteous. And she was possibly the clumsiest person he'd ever met on top of it all. He still couldn't help liking her.

And wanting to know what made her tick.

She claimed to be a mild-mannered antique dealer, but for someone in disguise, she was horribly see-through. He sensed a raw sexuality in Miss Witchiepoo that she would pretend to find shocking. He could see a siren inside those indignant, innocent eyes.

He pictured her at home with her geek fiancé. They probably liked to wear matching sweaters and expensive walking shoes. Probably went to the dentist every six months and checked the battery in their smoke detector daily. They probably had no idea what constituted a night of good sex, more than likely blocking out twenty minutes for it every Tuesday and Thursday nights. Hell, they probably didn't even sweat.

He couldn't help thinking it seemed like sort of a shame for a girl to have that much sexual energy inside her and be wasting it on someone who probably couldn't appreciate her. On someone who probably never even saw that side of her. She needed someone to coax it out of her, someone to show her that it was all right not to be so prim all the time. His heartbeat increased, knowing he could be that guy.

He knew he could set Julie free if she wanted him to. The sad thing, of course, was that she probably had no idea *what* she wanted. She probably had all these beautiful urges and no idea where they'd come from or what she should do with them. Damn that fiancé for not working harder to satisfy her.

And damn himself, too. What was he doing here anyway? Thinking about Witchiepoo way too hard, that was what. Fruitless. A total waste of time.

And she was really kind of ditzy anyway. Standing behind a cobweb at the party like it would make her invisible. Trampling those innocent mums. Inventing false careers for herself. All acts of pure silliness. And if he needed a woman in his life at all, which he didn't, it certainly wasn't one like that. After all, what kind of a woman thought Dino was a dog?

Still, it was hard to push down a certain fascination with her. And maybe she wasn't really so ditzy—maybe all those little oddities in her were cute. After all, if anyone liked a little silliness, it was him.

Nope, there was no getting rid of the way he wanted her right now. No taking his eyes off those nice round hips and the slim, curving waist above it. He considered asking her measurements out of curiosity, but thought better of it.

It was getting harder and harder being out there in the middle of nowhere with her. He smiled then, amused by his mental double entendre. But then his mind returned to all the things he wanted to do with her. And all he knew *she* wanted to do with him as well, no matter how she denied it.

"HUNGRY?" SCOTT ASKED her out of the blue.

She stopped and turned to face him, her heels lodging deeply in the dirt. "Kind of," she replied.

"Bit o' Honey?"

"What?"

"I think I have a Sugar Daddy too, if you'd prefer." He reached down into the hip of his costume and magically revealed a small handful of candy.

"You have a pocket in that thing?" she asked of his skin-tight suit.

"Yes, I have a pocket," he said as if mildly offended by the question. "Skeletons have to carry things, too. I picked up a handful of candy at the party. Must have been an omen—I must have known somehow that I'd be stuck out here and need snacks."

Julie surveyed the choices of candy in his outstretched palm. "Can I have the Kiss?" Then she felt her own blush. "The Hershey's Kiss, I mean."

"Take whatever you like," he said with a smile.

She hadn't realized how hungry she was. Only then did it occur to her that she hadn't had any dinner before the party, and even there she had only consumed a few chips and pretzels out of nervousness.

"Mind if we sit down a minute?" she asked. "My feet are getting achy."

He nodded and lowered himself onto the hardened dirt in the field, and she settled next to him. And when he offered his array of candy again, she quickly plucked the Hershey's Kiss from his hand. Speedily unwrapping it, she reached into the foil, ready to pop the candy into her mouth—only to have it ooze through her fingers. It was liquid chocolate.

"Yuck," she said. The gooey chocolate covered her fingers and a few thick droplets had splashed onto her chin when she'd tried to propel it toward her mouth. The rest of the candy had plopped down onto the bare swell of her right breast.

She flashed Scott a thick glare of disgust in time to see him gulp back a guilty swallow. "Guess it melted."

"Guess so," she replied sternly.

"Body heat," he concluded, offering a hopeful smile.

She didn't smile back, though. She could think of nothing besides how gooey she felt and how she hated to be caught without a napkin. "What am I gonna do about this mess?"

He hesitated, his eyes gentle and strange upon her, as if filled with vile thoughts somehow turned innocent. Unable to break free of his gaze, she felt something invisible changing, moving between them.

His voice came softly. "I'll clean you up."

And when he reached for Julie's hand, she trembled at his touch. Waiting for him to wipe her chocolaty fingers onto his sleeve or maybe even his leg, she couldn't stop quivering in anticipation of how it would feel. But instead he brought her hand to his mouth.

His lips closed gently around her index finger, making her gasp. Then he slowly sucked from the base of her finger to its tip, pulling it out clean but for the sticky moisture left by the chocolate and his mouth.

He gazed over at her, his eyes full of heat as his lips closed over another finger—and she thought briefly of strobe lights, deciding this was much better. His tongue circled the finger inside his mouth, licking the chocolate off slowly, each subtle movement triggering a bolt of excitement in the tender spot between her legs.

Scott continued to deliberately, sensuously clean each finger on her hand, the ache of desire gripping her tighter with each passing second. She'd never known such stimulation could move from her fingers through her entire body so quick and so strong, each touch from his tongue racing through her like a bolt of lightning.

"There," he said lowly, his voice a sexy rasp as he extracted the last finger from his mouth. "Hand's all clean now."

Once again trapped in his gaze, Julie could barely nod.

Then he whispered, "But your chin. There's chocolate on your chin."

And she knew she could stay quiet, maybe *should* stay quiet. Only she didn't want to. A blanket of warmth climbed her cheeks as she opened her mouth to whisper, "Lick it off."

The jolt of electricity assaulted him almost visibly. It showed in his fiery eyes and the sensual pout of his mouth in the moonlight. Until he slowly leaned forward, parting his lips slightly, then licking away the chocolate just below her lips.

And when he was done, the tip of his tongue moved upward, tracing the outline of her lips, making her heart shudder, making her want to kiss him again, kiss him like there was no tomorrow—but then he gently pulled back.

She wondered why, surprised and disappointed—only to see him open his eyes just long enough to make a brief, smoldering contact with hers before he lowered his gaze to the liquefied chocolate on her breast.

His head sank down then, his tongue pressing hotly onto the soft ridge of curved flesh. She gasped, then bit her lip as sensation reverberated through her whole body, setting it aflame. He drew his tongue away for just one excruciating second before letting it dip into the hollow between her breasts, the tip tracing a rivulet of chocolate that had dripped there. Then he softly lapped at the swelling rise of her breast again, heightening her desire with each lick.

When he finally lifted his face to hers, his breath was labored, his eyes wild.

And something in his hot, sexy gaze made Julie panic.

She couldn't be here, now, doing this. She couldn't want this man. Not this way. He wanted sex, not love, and she couldn't live with that. She'd wanted Patrick this badly and what had it gotten her? Heartache. Despair. A hundred different kinds of pain. It wasn't worth it—it simply wasn't.

"I can't," she breathed at him. "I just can't." She quickly rose from the ground and sprinted away from him as fast as her pumps would plod through the dirt. She kept her eyes focused on the rows of dead, broken cornstalks that carved the path before her and didn't look back.

Chapter Six

"JULIE! JULIE, WAIT!"

She ran as fast as her heels would allow until she finally realized how useless it was. They were stranded together in the middle of nowhere, after all. Where did she think she was going?

She slowed her pace, breathless and feeling stupid. Her heart beat so fast that it burned, ready to explode in her chest. She didn't know if it was the result of running so hard or from Scott's tongue licking her...

"Julie, I'm sorry," he said, reaching her.

He grabbed her wrist and she looked down at his hand. Still covered by tiny glowing bones and the fabric beneath, it felt no less warm and penetrating on her skin. Her gaze stayed fixed on his touch, and when he followed her eyes and realized her fear, he pulled back. Thank God, she thought in a strange mixture of desire and relief. His touch had been the very thing she'd been running from.

"I'm sorry," he said again. "I know you're...happily engaged. And I shouldn't have put you in that kind of position."

Despite her most fervent wishes, she couldn't respond. She couldn't yell at him; she couldn't even agree with him. Because even if he thought she was happily engaged, he still knew how she'd felt inside, knew how badly she'd hungered for his mouth on her skin. He probably knew how badly she still hungered for it *now*. For all of him.

His eyes locked onto hers, pleading for a response, perhaps forgiveness, or at least a pardon. Maybe he wanted her to scream at him; they argued well together and it kept the passion away, at least at intervals. But she couldn't do any of those things. And she feared that if she opened her mouth at all, it might be to pull him into a kiss.

Looking at him now, she no longer saw the glowing bones or the white and black makeup that concealed his face. She saw beyond that. She saw his eyes. His mouth. She heard his voice and felt his touch. She looked inside and saw his strength, his softness, his sense of humor. It was suddenly hard for Julie to believe she'd ever held faces in such reverence.

"Julie, are you okay?"

Again, he'd called her by name. Forgotten she was Witchiepoo. Had quit playing games. Games were cute. But this had gone beyond cute. At some point she couldn't pin down, it had passed from flirtation into a deep, almost ravenous desire.

"Julie?" he said again.

She couldn't believe how much she wanted him. Perhaps more than she'd ever wanted a man before. Even Patrick.

The realization hit her hard. She hadn't known that could happen. But suddenly it had. In the middle of a field. In the middle of the night. With a man whose face she couldn't see, didn't even *care* about seeing anymore.

She still feared speaking; she feared she would find herself spilling the horrible truth. *There is no boyfriend. I made him up. And I want you madly. More than your body. Your mind, your soul. But yes, definitely your body, too. I think I'm falling for you. And I can't fight my longings anymore.*

She darted her eyes about, panicky, searching for something, anything, to get her out of this bind. To take away her overwhelming desire, to calm the wild beating of her heart.

And then she saw it. In the distance. Through the trees. A shining beacon of rescue.

"A light," she whispered.

"What?"

She slowly lifted her hand to point behind him. "On the other side of those trees," she said without taking her eyes from the dim glowing dot. She feared that if she did, it might disappear.

Scott turned and peered through the dense foliage. Then, looking back to Julie, he took her hand. "Come on."

They set out at a brisk pace, crossing the cornfield,

weaving through the dead, used-up stalks until they reached the field's edge. When they moved onto unculti-vated ground, she stumbled into the waist-high grass, nearly losing her balance.

"Are you all right?" He placed a hand on her back to steady her. A big, warm, strong hand. A hand that she wanted to feel everywhere. It was far too dangerous.

"I'm fine," she said, stepping away from him, effec-tively pulling free of his touch. "Now let's quit wasting time."

She set out running in the direction of the light, moving through the tall, cool grass as fast as she could with the hindrances of her pumps and tight-to-the-knee dress. The sky had turned from black to gray and fell over her like a comforting shroud. The stars now hid themselves from view; only the bright shining eye of the moon guided her as she ran. She had to get away from Scott. She had to reach that light.

"Slow down," she heard him say somewhere behind her. "You're gonna break your leg and then what are we gonna do?"

But she ignored him. She had to get to that light, and soon. The proverbial beacon in the night, it symbol-ized safety. Freedom. From him. And all she wanted to do with him. If she stopped running, if she walked with him at a normal, civilized pace, she wasn't sure what would happen. She wasn't sure they'd make it to that light with their clothes on. Unready to deal with that possibility, she kept running.

"Hey, wait up," he called.

She glanced over her shoulder to see him jogging behind her beneath the gray blanket of sky. It fueled her even further and she accelerated. The sooner they reached that light, the better. It would save her from him. From herself. It would make life normal again. There would be no melty chocolate. There would be no locked doors. No uncertainty. No fear. The confusing darkness that had been clouding her vision for hours would finally be lifted.

She skidded down the hill into the valley that separated them from the light in the distance. Reaching it, she pulled her dress up over her knees, allowing her to step across the gully at the bottom, a small split in the land trickling with leftover rainwater from days before.

Once on the other side, she stopped to look over her shoulder. The glowing bones followed her and she knew he could see her standing there, her dress lifted to her thighs, watching him. Moonlight shone everywhere, the illumination of gray skies casting an eerie glow on the valley.

An image materialized in Julie's mind. She was lifting that dress, farther and farther, lifting it up all the way. Letting him look. Wanting him to see her. Taunting him with the prize. Taunting herself, too, with the distance she would keep between them.

But then the vision grew and the distance vanished. In her mind she could see him pushing her down in the tall grass, coming down on top of her, coming inside her.

She shuddered at the sensual picture in her mind. How long had she stood there just staring at him in the darkness? How long had she held his gaze and kept him grounded in place on the other side of that gully?

Weakness and longing held her in their grasp. How easy it would be to give in. To just lower herself down in that tall, dark grass and wait for him. He would come to her, she knew without doubt. He wouldn't ask questions. He would fill her up. She gasped at the thought.

Then she got hold of her senses and pushed her crazy thoughts aside.

She dropped the hem of her dress and began to run again, quickly moving up the hill that banked her side of the small valley.

SCOTT ALMOST WANTED to drop and beat his fists on the ground. What a horribly frustrating woman! He would have called her a tease, except he knew she wasn't being one on purpose. He knew it was still all that energy trying to fight its way free from inside her, trying to find its way out. God, how he'd felt it in her sweet breasts beneath his tongue. He had tasted her heartbeat.

Watching her run away from him had felt like being stranded alone in a desert without a drop of water to quench him.

And then he'd seen her, standing across the valley from him, that pure passion lingering on her face, her eyes locked on him like tiny diamonds beneath the moonlight.

Both times she'd almost let go. Almost, but not quite.

He imagined chasing her, catching up to her, pushing her down into the grass. Giving her what he knew she ached for. Only he wasn't that kind of a guy. Never had been, never could be. She had to want him and she had to *know* she wanted him. Nothing else would work.

He thought of the stripper back at the party. Some girl taught how to dance sexy and play with men's minds in order to earn a large paycheck. Julie, of course, hadn't understood his lack of interest in a woman freely shedding her clothes. And he hadn't bothered telling her that such forced, pretend sex held no fire for him—its falseness distorted what he thought of as good, pure, hot sexuality. It hadn't been appropriate to try to explain something like that to Witchiepoo back at the party. He'd already offended her enough with too much talk of sex by that time, and he doubted she would have believed such an explanation anyway.

But when he'd seen her across the valley with her dress hiked up, playing with him, waiting for him to pursue her just so she could run away again, *then* he'd thought of telling her, of explaining to her why strippers and centerfolds and the whole sex industry just wasn't his bag. Because none of it was real.

But Julie was real. The message she'd been sending as she'd stood there beckoning to him with her shimmering eyes—that was real. And what she'd made him feel inside—that was real, too. A little *too* real at the moment. He only wished he could make her understand, could somehow take her fear away.

He finally crossed the tiny stream that rippled through the valley where everything had stood so still for one horrible, lovely moment. And upon reaching the spot where she'd stood taunting him, he sighed.

He needed to give up on this, he knew. She wasn't going to give in to her wants, give in to *him*. Instead, she would hold it all in and be faithful to a man who obviously didn't have what it took to make her happy.

Slowly trudging through the high grass, he realized that he couldn't see her anywhere ahead of him. Damn it, where on earth had she run off to? He picked up his own pace then until he was jogging. Passion aside, they still needed to stick together out there in the dark.

JULIE QUICKLY DISCOVERED that running uphill was much harder than coming down had been. Especially in those damn heels. She considered just ditching them there, finally freeing herself of them, but just as quickly realized that she needed them to protect her feet.

She grew breathless, praying to find the light soon. A furtive glance over her shoulder revealed Scott approaching, suddenly moving up quickly behind her. Apparently the hill didn't bother him. Apparently those hiking boots were paying off. She only wished *she'd* have chosen such appropriate shoes for a night of true hell.

For the first time since darting away from his touch, she slowed her pace to a walk—because she had no other choice. Her chest felt as if it would soon explode with exhaustion and her feet throbbed in pain. She could only imagine how reddened her poor toes must be, and she knew blisters crowned both heels. She wanted to collapse.

Scott said nothing when he finally caught up with her. Angry, she supposed. Or maybe just confused. Who could blame the guy? Another vision filled her mind then, and this one, unlike her fantasy in the valley, was real. It was Scott's head buried in her cleavage. Scott's tongue licking chocolate from her breast.

She pulled in her breath, fighting the horrible, exquisite physical reaction that the memory triggered. And she wished she could run away from him all over again, but exhaustion prevented it.

"Still got that Bit o' Honey?" she said, breaking the silence.

He nodded and extracted the remaining candy from his pocket. "I don't think those melt."

Julie took it from his hand and peeled off the wrapper, letting it waft away in the passing breeze.

"Litterbug," he muttered.

"Sorry, nature boy," she snapped, "but I'm fresh out of trash cans."

He rolled his eyes in response, leaving her to feel her obvious overreaction, as she popped the candy into her mouth, thankful for the rush of taste that instantly woke her up. Then she resumed walking silently, slowly, up the hill, letting Scott take the lead.

What am I doing? Why have I been running so hard? And why do I consistently have to make him mad?

She herself had almost begun to believe that she had a boyfriend, that it was the reason she couldn't let herself want Scott. The real truth, though, was that she couldn't let herself love that kind of man again. A man who wouldn't commit, a man who wanted nothing more than a romp in the hay—or the field, as the case may be. She couldn't let herself get hurt that way again, couldn't let herself fall in love with a man who wouldn't love her back.

Still, the image of Scott's mouth on her sensitive skin returned. And she found herself thinking again about how easy it would be to just give in. To just lie down. Right here—in the tall, soft grass. Under the huge glowing moon.

Not just to imagine it, like down in the valley, but to really do it. To let him take her in his arms. Hold her. Touch her. Move inside her. Then fall asleep there. In the middle of nowhere.

It sounded beautiful to Julie. Even if he couldn't promise her love. Or commitment. Even if he couldn't promise her anything more than the rest of this night.

Grow up. Follow Rhonda's advice. For once in your life, be a big girl. Do what you want. What feels right. Patrick had been wild, but everything wild didn't have to be Patrick. Everything wild didn't have to be bad.

Julie drew in her breath and stepped slowly up behind Scott as he plodded forward. She moved close enough to touch him, to pull him into her arms. Close enough to whisper the truth in his ears.

Her stomach churned with fear, but her heart beat madly with desire.

And then she slowly began to reach out her hand.

"There," he said. His glowing fingers pointed the way. "The light. See it?"

The words made her release a thick sigh of disappointment. That damn beacon of rescue had just come back into view after the long and arduous climb. "I see it," she whispered softly.

Then he looked back at her, his painted face shining in the moonlight. "What's wrong?" he asked. "We're almost there. Home free."

And she nodded, but obviously not convincingly enough.

"I thought that's what you wanted," he said. "You were certainly running toward it hard enough."

She just swallowed. "It *is* what I wanted," she told him. "It's exactly what I wanted." Then she sucked in her breath and peered straight ahead as she tentatively set off walking toward the light and away from Scott. Her moment of bravery had passed. And now there seemed to be nothing else to do but push on toward the goal.

As she moved closer and the light grew larger, she could see that it emerged from the window of a small, weathered farmhouse that would have otherwise simply blended in to the bleak rural landscape. Pumpkins of all sizes appeared to weigh down the sagging front porch—and behind the house set a barn, a small tractor by its side. A sleeping dog lay curled up on the tractor's seat.

But Julie slowed her pace as she approached the house. She'd pushed aside her silly thoughts on the hillside and had returned to the mode of being anxious to go home and call it a night, yet it suddenly felt a little dangerous to march up to a stranger's house in the middle of nowhere. She stopped walking as Scott continued briskly past her. What felt so eerie about this house? She knew it made no sense, but…

"Wait, wait, wait," she whispered, rushing up behind him.

"What?" he whispered back, stopping.

"Be careful of that dog," she cautioned. "Don't wake him up."

"Why? He won't hurt us. Look at him—he's Tramp."

"I wasn't worried so much about getting attacked as I was about him barking his head off and letting the people in the house know we're out here."

"Not a problem," he told her. "Because *I'm* about to let them know we're out here, without Tramp's help." He started again toward the small house, taking bold strides.

"What do you think you're doing?" she groused, rushing up behind him and grabbing his wrist.

Scott couldn't recall her having done that before—

initiating a touch. And it felt good. Very good. And though he didn't exactly think his actions needed an explanation, he decided to humor her anyway.

"Well," he explained, "I'm gonna knock on that door and ask the people inside if I can use their phone."

"Just like that?" she asked, her eyes wide.

He let his brow knit. "Just like *what*? Of course just like that."

"I think we should take a look around first."

"Why?" he asked impatiently. What had gotten into her all of a sudden?

"Just to see what kind of people we're dealing with here," she told him. "This doesn't exactly look like the Brady house."

Scott glanced around, exaggerating the activity. "Gee, looks like people who farm, people who have a dog." Noting the neglected remains of a flowerbed, he added, "People who aren't big on yard work. But I'm sure they're perfectly Brady people. Even if it doesn't exactly show."

"Not too big on home repair, either," she pointed out as if it were a crime—and he followed her eyes to discover a shutter hanging by one hinge.

"Okay, not big into home repair. Does that about answer all your questions?"

"Not exactly," she replied, readopting her worried tone. "Look, we've come this far. There's nothing wrong with a little caution."

He let out a sigh and she shot him a look of annoyance. And so he steeled his determination and marched right past her anyway. He hadn't come this far just to stand around and wait for the sun to rise.

He strolled up onto the porch, Julie on his heels. Then he lifted his hand to knock on the old wooden door frame, but she reached around to grab his wrist again, whispering, "Scott, wait!"

"Why?" he boomed, spinning to face her.

He met wildly alarmed eyes as she commanded, "Shhhh!" with a finger to her lips.

He dropped his voice to an annoyed whisper. "What's wrong with you?"

"Look in that window," she instructed him with a glance to the left, her voice low, but edged with something close to panic.

And even as he strode a few steps toward the window from which the light glowed, her arm shot out to stop his progress. "Slowly," she warned. "Quiet. There's a man in there watching TV."

He flashed her a skeptical glance, then stole nearer the window, finally peeking inside. An old man relaxed his heavy frame in a tattered reclining chair, a bowl of ice cream in his lap. He wore a once-red flannel shirt beneath a pair of denim overalls and his eyes were set intently on the television set, the screen casting a dull glare across the room.

"Looks safe enough to me," Scott whispered over his shoulder.

"Does he look familiar to you or anything?" Her tone

was filled with foreboding.

"No," he said. "Why would he?"

"I just think I've seen him, that's all."

"Yeah? Where?"

She swallowed nervously, her eyes grave. "On TV."

And Scott leaned forward slightly, confused and ready to get to the bottom of this. He wished she'd just spit it out already, whatever *it* was. "What was he on TV for?"

"Scott," she said, "I'm not sure, but I could swear that's Daryl Dukes."

"Daryl Dukes?" he asked. Where had he heard that name?

"You know, the old guy who killed his family a long time ago? The guy who escaped from a mental hospital a few weeks back and is still on the loose?"

Scott blinked. Now he remembered—he'd seen the guy on TV just last night. He forced himself to stay calm. "Oh. That Daryl Dukes."

"I saw a report about him earlier tonight," she said. "Police are starting to link him with those two college girls that got murdered last week and there's a missing pizza delivery guy they think he might've gotten, too."

Now it was Scott who swallowed nervously, trying to weigh all this, and trying to crush back the fresh sense of horror sizzling up his spine. Could it be? Could the man sitting only a few feet away from them be a serial killer? Damn, he'd been so ready to knock on this door. What the hell were they going to do now?

Julie's stomach twisted. Now she wished they'd stayed back at the haunted house, back where the dangers were only pretend. How safe they'd been there without even realizing it.

The eerie silence was broken when a dog's howl cut through the night—and her eyes shot open wide to meet the new panic revealed in Scott's.

"We should get out of here," he said.

"The sooner the better," she agreed.

But Tramp howled again, this time louder, and more intently, the sound filling the night air all around them. Then the porch light flicked on and Julie turned just in time to see the door open. An ominous shadow filled the narrow rectangle of light.

"Run!" Scott yelled.

Julie leaped from the porch. She tripped on the last wooden step, but regained her balance and took off in a sprint.

"Hey!" Daryl Dukes said behind her. "Hey, you come back here! Come back here right now!"

When she heard the screen door slam, she knew Daryl Dukes had exited the house. He was probably going to chase them down. Serial killers probably loved it when victims showed up right on their doorsteps and saved them the trouble of going out. Like that poor pizza delivery guy. "Come back here!" he yelled again.

She instinctively reached down to lift her dress over her knees to help her take longer strides, to move farther faster, her heart rising to her throat. She ran without foresight or direction, much like earlier in the haunted house when she'd been escaping the man with the ax in his head. But this time her flight held much more importance.

She wondered where Scott was, yet couldn't look around for fear that it would slow her progress. She ran recklessly, her course making her dizzy—even more so when a glance down showed her the ground moving beneath her at jagged angles with incredible speed.

Getting farther from the house and the light, it became difficult to see, and she glanced up only long enough to find that a misty gray-white cloud had floated into the moon's path and now obscured its bright light, too. She ran aimlessly, praying for safety. The voice of Daryl Dukes continued to ring out behind her in the distance, but the words had grown indecipherable. She tried to blink away tears as she ran.

That was when the ground dropped out from under her. And she found herself sliding through a carpet of loudly crushing leaves down a steep incline until—*plunk*, her hip met roughly with a tree trunk. An involuntary moan left her at the crash.

She lay unmoving on the ground in the darkness, only vaguely aware of pain. And when she finally opened her eyes, she found herself staring upward, focusing on the thin hint of the moon visible through the naked treetops above. Apparently she had tumbled into a thick grove of trees.

She sat up slowly, more leaves crunching beneath her

as she moved, and she scooted a bit, moving her aching hip away from the killer tree trunk. But when she attempted to stand, her ankle gave out beneath her, a sharp pain shooting up her leg. She fell to the ground with a thud.

Where on earth was Scott? And how would he ever find her stuck down here?

She scolded herself for how stupid she'd been. Running off in the darkness without even keeping an eye on him? It wouldn't have been hard to follow his movements—he glowed, for heaven's sake. But it certainly would have been much harder for him to see where *she* had gone. Her dress was black as the night. No wonder they hadn't ended up in the same place.

And then a horrible realization suddenly invaded Julie's head. She gasped and lifted a hand to her heart. Scott glowed—his movements would have been easy to follow. Not just for her. But for Daryl Dukes as well.

She trembled, her eyes suddenly welling with tears. Oh, God, what if…? She couldn't even finish the thought.

Weakened still more by stark fear, she collapsed back into the dead leaves, then pulled her hands up to her face to help muffle her sobs.

Her ankle throbbed with a thick, dull pain. And so did her hip. She was stuck in the middle of the woods a million miles from nowhere in the middle of the night. And now Scott—sweet, funny, sexy Scott…

No. It can't be. It just can't.

Then she began to pray. *Please let him be all right. Please let him be all right and please let him find me. Please get us home, God. Please just get us home.*

Chapter Seven

———— ∞ ————

SCOTT WAS NOT prone to fear. Unlike Julie, it took more than a few imaginary monsters in a haunted house to send him screaming into the night.

No, it took a raving lunatic like Daryl Dukes.

The only problem was that Scott hadn't kept his eye on Julie. Now he paced back and forth across an empty ridge, his chest tight with worry. How on earth had he lost track of her? What kind of imbecile lost a beautiful woman in the dark in the middle of nowhere?

He'd grown frustrated from calling her name over and over and getting no reply. He had also developed a fear of attracting Daryl Dukes with his voice, so he kept his calls to a hoarse whisper. No wonder she couldn't hear him. Still, every few minutes he cried out for her in that same low voice, wishing it were safe to shout. How else would he ever find her? Who even knew how far apart they might have drifted? His stomach filled with dread.

"Julie! Julie, where are you! Do you hear me, Julie?"

Again no answer came, and his heart plummeted.

Each reply of silence sent a sharp pain shooting through his chest. Where could she be?

He knew her well enough by now to know that wherever she was, she was petrified. And he wouldn't let himself think about the possibility that something had happened to her. She had to be out there somewhere looking for him, too. She had to be.

He swallowed hard, a lump in his throat. Okay, he had to admit it, he was really getting worried now. "Where the hell could she be?" he asked the moon. But he knew in his heart that it was more than worry, more than a simple one-human-being-to-another kind of concern. God help him, he'd started to care about this woman. And he had to find her.

JULIE ROSE GINGERLY to a sitting position, then peeled a leaf from her cheek, stuck there, she supposed, from her tears. She thought of Scott. And of Daryl Dukes. And the horrible stabbing pain washed over her anew.

Only then she heard it. A faint cry in the distance echoing its way through the trees. "Julie! Where are you, Julie?" His voice, though far off and muffled, sounded desperate.

She opened her mouth to call back to him, but stopped. What if this was a trick? What if Daryl Dukes held Scott at gunpoint or knifepoint or something, and had forced him to yell out her name? Was it possible that even as he called for her he hoped she wouldn't answer?

As his voice grew nearer, she became steeped in confusion. She couldn't think rationally anymore. And even as terrified as she was, she could no longer ignore his pleas.

"Scott!" she yelled into the night. It came out weaker than she'd intended. So much of her strength had faded. So she called out again. "Scott!"

"Where are you, Julie?"

His voice seemed to echo from overhead, probably from the ridge she'd toppled off of. "Down in the trees," she called back. "I'm hurt."

"Hurt?" His voice, now closer, came from right above her. And when she turned her head in the direction from which it came, her heart filled with joy at the sight of those glowing bones.

"Down here," she called. "Right below you."

His footsteps increased in nearness and speed as he jogged toward her through the fallen leaves, the bones growing thankfully closer. And upon reaching her, he dropped to his knees at her side.

Suddenly having him that close to her again, after she'd feared the worst, pushed all thoughts of physical pain from her mind. She could think only of the terror she'd suffered while they'd been apart. And of the incredible relief flowing through her body at his return. Despite the pain in her ankle and hip when she moved, she flung her arms around his neck. She hadn't planned it, but she couldn't stop it either.

His arms circled her lightly, tentatively.

And she followed the urge to bury her face in his glowing chest, thankful for the warmth of his sturdy body and for the arms that strengthened their hold on her now. Fresh tears sprung from her eyes.

"Julie, honey, what's wrong? What am I missing here?" His breath felt hot on her ear.

"I just thought," she stammered through her tears, "that Daryl Dukes…got you."

"Oh."

She gazed up into his warm brown eyes, so full of compassion and understanding. Then she tightened her grip around his neck.

"Don't worry, honey," he said. "I'm all right. I just ran like hell. I thought you were right behind me the whole time. And when I realized that you weren't…"

"Do you think," she asked nervously, "that he could be…looking for us?"

Scott's embrace stiffened at the awful question. "I…I don't know."

And the silence grew so deafening that she had to fill it. "I banged my hip pretty hard," she told him. "But the real problem is my ankle. I can't walk."

She saw him pull in his breath before he reached down, slipping his fabric-covered hand beneath the flared hem of her dress to run his fingers gently over her ankle.

"Ouch." She winced at the touch that, under other circumstances, would have felt so nice.

"Sorry," he said, pulling back his hand. "You've got a hell of a bump down there."

She leaned into his chest again—it was beginning to be the only place she felt safe. "Scott," she finally whispered, "what are we gonna do?"

After a long moment punctuated with only the eerie hoot of an owl somewhere in the distance, he finally answered, "Maybe we should give up for a while. Just stay here for the night. And in the morning, when we can see, I'll carry you out of here."

Julie sighed with mixed emotions. The sweetness of the gesture warmed her heart, but the practicality of the issue couldn't be ignored. "You can't carry me all that way. We don't even know where we are, but we know that wherever this is, it's miles back to where we came from."

"That's all right," he whispered.

"What do you mean?"

"Look, the only other way to get help would be for me to leave you here alone. And I'm not about to do that, especially with that nut out there somewhere."

"It's getting cold," she murmured, realizing for the first time that she'd started to shiver. Maybe it had taken lying in the leaves for a while to make her aware of the chill.

"I'll try to keep you warm," he offered, pulling her closer, then rubbing his hands vigorously over her back in an effort to ward off the cold.

She looked up then, into his eyes—and noticed for the first time that a spot of blood dotted his forehead. She gasped gently. "You're bleeding."

"Am I?" he asked matter-of-factly.

"Your forehead."

"I walked into a tree branch a while back," he informed her. "No biggie."

When she reached up to dab at the blood with her fingertips, he hissed at the touch. "Sorry," she whispered.

Then she glanced down at her fingers in the moonlight, at Scott's blood. And also at the white paint smudged upon them. Looking back at him, she saw that the spot where the blood had been now appeared flesh-colored. She pulled in her breath at the first sight of his skin.

"What?" he asked.

"Nothing," she replied.

"I was worried sick about you," he blurted then, his voice suddenly frantic with grief.

"Huh?"

"When I couldn't find you, Julie, I...I..."

"What?" she whispered.

He shook his head, unable to provide words. Then he sighed. "If anything had happened to you, I'd never have forgiven myself."

"But...why?" she asked softly. "I mean, we only met a few hours ago. You hardly know me."

Scott's eyes radiated heat. "Yes," he said, "I do."

"What?"

"I *do* know you. I *must* know you. How could I care about you so much if I didn't?" His eyes, softening, shone so warmly that they seemed liquid brown.

Had she heard him correctly? Her lips trembled as she spoke. "You…care about me?"

"More than I should," he whispered.

"More than you should?" She shook her head. "Scott, what does that mean?"

He sighed. "You know I try to steer clear of that sort of thing these days. That I'm not looking for a relationship. And besides," he added, "you're taken."

"Oh yeah," she said, remembering the lie. That stupid, idiotic lie. How she wanted to take it back now and tell him the truth about her boyfriend, or lack thereof. But how could she explain her actions? Fear, loneliness, wishful thinking? She couldn't bear to envision what he would think of her if he found out she'd been lying to him all this time for absolutely no good reason. Besides which, she couldn't think straight right now—she was too busy trying to fight too many other feelings.

Their faces lingered so closely that she could feel his breath on her cheek, could feel the way it slowly accelerated, coming deeper, harder. She bit her lip, once again trying to push away all the desire he instilled in her.

But this time the desire pushed back. It pushed through the ache in her hip and the pain in her ankle. It pushed through her fear for their fate. It pushed through the weakness that had previously consumed her. Her body tingled with want.

"Scott," she said warmly, "kiss me."

And his breath trembled in her ear. "What?" he asked, obviously surprised.

"Kiss me," she repeated. "Please. Please kiss me."

She heard his impassioned sigh, then felt his lips brush against her cheek. She turned her mouth toward his and their lips met in a moment of soft, silent exploration.

Then the hot pressure of his mouth on hers increased as they sank together into a kiss so deep that it reverberated through her toes. She tentatively spread her lips to offer him her tongue—and he licked at it with a soft, darting motion before fully circling it with his own.

A gentle rhapsody of raindrops began to softly spatter Julie's cheeks as Scott's mouth melded with hers. The soft drizzle soon wet lips and dampened clothes.

She wanted to sit in the leaves and kiss him that way forever, rain or no rain. In fact, her desire swelled with the trickle of the raindrops—she wanted to get wet with him. Roll in damp leaves with him. Melt into the pungent earth with their movements.

But the shower soon got heavier, growing uncomfortably colder. "We need to get out of the rain," he whispered. "I saw an old broken down school bus up on the ridge above us."

"But I can't walk," she reminded him.

"Shhh," he said. And then he scooped her up into his capable arms.

She hugged him, comforted by the warmth his body provided even as he carried her through the cold rain. It felt delicious to be in his grasp, in his care, and she held on to him as tightly as she could.

As they exited the trees, the silhouette of an old bus appeared. It rested alone near the top of the hill on a rusting yellow frame, no tires. As the rain fell increasingly harder, Scott ran the last few yards, even with Julie in his arms—and reaching the front door of the old bus, he kicked it inward, TV cop fashion.

An acrid odor bit at her nose as he carried her up the steps. Stale, mildewed air. But at least it was dry. And warm. It served as a safe haven, not only from the rain outside, but from all that had happened to them throughout this crazy night.

"Not exactly *The Partridge Family* bus," Scott said, "but it'll do."

"Maybe a coat of paint in a few wild colors would help?" Julie offered with a soft smile.

"And a few thousand air fresheners," he added.

She expected him to lower her into a seat near the front of the bus, but instead, he proceeded farther down the aisle, careful not the bang her sprained ankle against any of the old brown vinyl seats. "Where are we going?" she asked.

His expression was the most playful she'd seen in a while. "Everybody knows that if you're going to make out on the bus, you do it in the back seat."

She grinned up at him. "Are we going to make out?"

"Unless you tell me no."

She hesitated for only a second, then nuzzled closer against his chest.

He carefully lowered himself into the last seat of the

bus, resting her legs across his lap, her back propped comfortably against the window, and she found herself glancing down at the back of the seat in front of them. Inked obscenities and long-ago phone numbers of high school girls sporting bad reputations covered the vinyl, and elaborate ink hearts surrounded the names of youthful lovers. Julie absently reached one slim finger up to trace a large heart belonging to *Robin and Jim*.

"I don't think anyone ever wrote my name in a heart on a bus seat or wrote 'Julie times anybody' anywhere," she murmured.

"Girl thing, honey," he whispered sweetly. "Guys don't do the heart bit."

Made sense, she thought, sighing. "Guess not." How naive she remained, even at thirty.

"Unless, of course," Scott added, "a guy is getting ready to put the moves on a girl. Then he might do the heart thing. Strictly as a kiss-up, though."

She nodded and they both stayed quiet, thinking.

"If I had a pen," he offered in a whisper, "I'd do the heart thing for you."

And a soft flutter wafted through her chest. "Really?" Then she remembered what he'd just said. "Because you're ready to put the moves on me, though. Right?"

"Yes," he said. Then quickly, "No. I mean, I am. But I would do it anyway."

"I thought guys didn't do the heart bit," she reminded him.

"Well, it takes quite a woman to make us want to

commit our name in ink on a school bus seat, but every now and then," he said with a sweet, sexy grin, "one comes along."

Julie flushed with the warmth and tenderness that come with a fresh, new romance. Scott had a way of taking her back to a long time ago, a distant place; he had a way of making her feel like a teenager again.

She reached up to run her hand through his thick, dark hair, now damp from the rain. And she gazed at his face, the moon shining in a nearby window to illuminate it for the first time since they'd climbed onto the bus. Then she gasped slightly at what she saw. More skin.

"What?" he asked her.

"Your makeup is starting to wash off. From the rain." She couldn't actually see *much* of his face, but thin, flesh-colored rivulets now streaked the white and black paint she'd grown so accustomed to. Reaching up, she extended one finger to touch a thick band of clean skin on his cheek—yet then pulled her hand back abruptly.

"What's wrong?" he asked. "Don't you want to see what I look like?"

"No," she said, surprising herself with such unbridled honesty. "Not really."

"Afraid you won't like what you see?"

"That's not it," she said, sad he would think that.

"What then?"

She tried to sort out her feelings as she spoke. "Maybe it's because that white and black paint is like…a safety wall between us."

His eyes narrowed as he whispered, "What does that mean?"

"Have you ever spent a lot of time talking to someone on the phone without knowing what they look like?" she asked, trying to make him understand. "And then when you actually meet them, it's so different. It can be so awkward. You think you've gotten to know someone, and yet there's this whole physical side to them that's completely new.

"Or maybe," she went on, "it's because it really doesn't *matter* to me what you look like anymore. That I don't want to know because I don't even care. Earlier it was driving me crazy wondering what your face was like underneath that paint. But somewhere along the way, Scott, I realized I'd be crazy about you no matter *what* you look like."

Like all night, one thing his costume couldn't hide was the expression in his eyes, and she read the passion etched there just before he brought his mouth down on hers. She let herself sink fully and completely into his kiss, at first soft, then turning slowly ravenous. When his teeth nibbled gently, hotly, at her lips, a tender moan escaped her—and she laid back her head, wanting to feel him *everywhere*.

His kisses sank to her neck as his hand moved deftly up from her waist, slowly rising to cup the side of her breast. He molded gently, kneading her soft flesh, and she teemed with desire, wanting more. Each caress, each kiss to her sensitive skin, escalated her excitement.

Soon enough, breath grown labored, he leaned down to softly kiss the curving slopes of her heaving breasts, revealed by the low-cut dress. She closed her eyes and released a soft moan at the exquisite sensation that shot to her panties. She wanted him, more, deeper, and she arched her back to further lift her breasts to his mouth. She longed for his kisses everywhere.

When his mouth began working at the tight fabric covering one hardened nipple, she hissed with heat. And he bit softly through the dress, sending an explosion of pleasure through her body. "Oh Scott," she whispered, pleading for more.

She opened her eyes and watched his fingers tugging at the fabric that covered her breasts, trying to pull the dress down. But—for heaven's sake—the too-tight material would barely budge! He tugged again, and the material strained but wouldn't give. As their gazes met, he clenched his teeth and let his eyes widen in frustration.

He moved his hand swiftly downward then, apparently trying to approach the problem from another angle. Sliding his fabric-covered fingers beneath the hem of her dress, his hand found her knee and proceeded to glide upward onto her thigh. A thrilling wave of heat followed, rising even higher than his hand.

But he released another sigh of frustration when he could move his fingers no farther, stopped again by the dress's tight fit near the tops of her thighs.

"You know, I used to love this dress," he told her,

"but I'm beginning to hate it now." Then he flashed a speculative look her way. "If only I were Plasticman."

"Who?"

"You remember. He could bend his body, or a part of it, into any shape to suit a given situation. For instance, if I were Plasticman, I'd flatten my arm out like a spatula so I could slide it up under this dress. Or better yet," he said, one glowing finger in the air, then lifting another to make a cutting motion, "I'd turn this arm into a big pair of scissors and I'd snip this dress right off of you."

Which prompted her to suggest, "You could just reach behind my back and unzip it, you know."

"You would let me do that?" He arched one eyebrow. "I thought gradual seduction techniques might be more effective."

"Scissors are not exactly gradual," she whispered hotly.

"No," he said with a wink, "but once I put them to work on the dress, you wouldn't have much of a choice then, would you?"

Julie pulled in her breath, desire filling her body with hunger and turning her reckless—and she gazed up at him, aware of the heat that filled her eyes. "I don't care how you do it, Scott," she said, "I just want you to make love to me."

The words made his jaw drop.

And while a part of her was equally surprised, she only cast him a small smile to say, "Don't look so shocked. It's blowing your sexy demeanor."

Though in response, his grin took on a deliciously seductive edge. "It takes more than a little shock to blow my sexy demeanor," he informed her.

"But…just one more thing," she said softly. "I need to feel your hands."

"What?" he murmured.

"They've been covered with that costume all night. I need to feel them on me. Skin to skin."

"No problem," he said. And then he reached beneath the wrist of his right arm and gave a firm yank. The seam split nicely and his hand was free. He smoothly did the same to the left arm and the sound of the fabric ripping sent an extra swirl of excitement rippling through Julie's core.

He lifted both hands to her face then, caressing her cheeks, then letting her lightly kiss his fingers before they passed down over her neck, finally coming to rest on the exposed ridge of her breasts. She sighed and closed her eyes. His hands were wonderful. His touch electric. She wanted to bathe in it.

But without warning, something in that touch turned suddenly rigid, his hands remaining tense and unmoving too long. She opened her eyes to see him peering past her out into the rain and the darkness beyond.

"What is it?" she asked.

"Listen," he whispered. "Do you hear something?"

She sat up a little, placing her hand on top of the seat

in front of them for balance. And above the pattering of the rain on the bus roof, she could faintly hear an engine, the sound of a vehicle. Her stomach began to quiver.

Yet as quickly as she heard it, the noise died away.

"Just a passing car?" she asked hopefully.

But Scott didn't seem convinced. "Shhh," he cautioned her. "Keep listening."

And then they both heard it. A low, sharp trill in the distance. The sound of someone whistling. *Oh Susanna.* Somewhere out in the darkness. The sound moved gradually nearer.

Julie laced her arms around Scott's neck and he tightened his grip at her waist. Something about that lone human sound descending upon them in the darkness was undeniably eerie, making her shiver in his grasp.

"Look," he whispered. And even before she turned her head, she dreaded what she would see.

Out the bus window, a light moved gently toward them. One single, slow-moving beam.

Just a flashlight, obviously. Held by a man who was whistling.

It shouldn't be ominous.

But it was.

They didn't speak a word or move a muscle.

Julie struggled to catch her breath as she attempted to accept her terror, accept her fate.

Next to her, Scott reached down to the back door of the bus beside their seat—the emergency exit—and pushed down the handle. But she knew what would happen. Nothing. Rusted shut. There was nowhere to run.

And the light had grown too close now to think about escaping through the front of the bus. Even if she *could* have walked.

The frantic beating of her heart seemed to keep time with the whistler's tune, growing louder and louder. The light lingered just beyond the door now, and the rain had lightened. Scott's fingers dug desperately into her skin.

They watched in helpless silence as the same man they'd seen earlier climbed up into the bus, flashlight in hand. He moved slowly but deliberately, his face expressionless. The light flickered about the bus, but it landed quickly on the inhabitants of the back seat—and there it stayed, their fear spotlighted.

Julie felt like a deer frozen in headlights, unable to move. The backlighting of the flashlight's beam cast a deadly pallor over Daryl Dukes' sagging face as he stopped whistling to let his mouth spread into a sinister smile. The sudden silence was deafening as his narrowed eyes locked on Julie and Scott's embrace.

"Well, well, well," he said with an evil laugh, "what do we got us here?"

Chapter Eight

HEARING THE EVIL chill in the man's voice, Julie pressed instinctively closer against Scott. It reminded her of every psycho/slasher movie she'd ever seen, but worse. This was a man who killed for the mere pleasure of killing. This was what she had *really* feared inside the haunted house. She couldn't have imagined how horrifyingly close true terror lay.

Scott tightened his grip on her, as well—then bravely lifted his eyes to the man walking toward them down the aisle. "Listen," he said, "do whatever you want with me, it doesn't matter. Just let her go."

And even in the midst of stark fear, her heart swelled with love. Finding out that Scott would put her life before his, that he would give himself up to win her freedom, hit her with more strength than anything anyone had ever done for her. She wished that they'd made love.

She was shaken from her regret, though, when Daryl Dukes took another forbidding step forward, then stopped, only three seats from where they huddled.

"What the Sam Hill you talkin' about, son?" he asked.

The man seemed genuinely confused.

And Scott's expression grew just as befuddled.

And Julie wondered if murderers often called their victims-to-be by such endearments as *son*.

"I'm asking you not to hurt her," Scott finally said. He spoke slowly, and she knew they were both thinking the same thing: Maybe the man was so crazy that he simply didn't understand.

Daryl Dukes laughed in reply—but it wasn't a menacing, evil laugh like she expected. No, it was more of a good-hearted belly laugh. "Why on earth would I hurt anybody?" he asked. "Just come out here to see if you folks was in trouble, that's all."

"Um," Scott began, "you aren't…Daryl Dukes?"

And again the big man let out a chuckle, this time using his free hand to clutch at his wide stomach. "Hell no," he said. "My name's Melvin."

Then a small woman stepped up onto the bus behind him, pushing back the hood of a yellow rain slicker to reveal a kind, elderly face below a head of white hair.

"Come on in here, Clara," Melvin said, "and tell these kids I ain't that Daryl Dukes serial killer fella."

Clara smiled consolingly as she made her way back the aisle to stand behind Melvin. "This old fool?" she asked, offering a wink. "I can't even get him to kill a chicken for Sunday dinner."

Scott and Julie stared at the old couple, dumbfounded, as Melvin laughed at his wife's little joke. "T'aint the first time somebody thought that, though, is it, Clara? Why, last week I was shoppin' over to the Piggly Wiggly, mindin' my own business, when somebody called the cops. They come stealin' up the bread aisle at me from both ends. I had to go down to the station for question-in' and ever'thing, didn't I, Clara? Rode in the back seat of their police car, even, with that screen up between us like I was a real dangerous fella. All in all, a pretty entertainin' afternoon."

Julie tried to smile, but she couldn't. She was still trying to quell her terror and come back to reality. Scott's fingers continued to dig just as tightly into her skin and she suspected he had the same problem.

"You kids scared the blazes outta me back there on my porch," Melvin went on.

Then Scott finally found his voice again. "You scared us pretty bad, too. How'd you find us?" he asked. "And *why'd* you find us?"

"Well," Melvin began, "when I stood on my porch and seen a glowin' skeleton go sprintin' acrost my field, I figured either the hants finally come fer me or somebody needed help. Clara's the kind-hearted one, and when I told her, she figured on the latter. We took out drivin' and seen them bones climb up on my old bus here."

"I brought some cookies," Clara said, holding out a clear plastic bag. "Figure if you're all the way out here on foot, you gotta be tired and you gotta be hungry."

Scott sighed. "We are," he admitted. "We went to a

haunted house earlier tonight and accidentally got locked inside. We saw the light in your window and came to use the phone, but…" he stopped.

"But you thunk I was that serial killer fella on the loose."

"Yeah," he said, sounding a little embarrassed now. "Then Julie hurt her leg, and it started to rain, and we saw your flashlight coming closer, and—"

"Here," Clara said, holding out the bag again, "have a cookie."

Julie didn't really want a cookie—having the life scared out of her had pushed down her appetite. But she reached out and took the bag from Clara anyway. "Thank you," she whispered.

"That rickety old haunted house is a good four miles from here as the crow flies," Clara told them. "It's amazin' y'all made it this far on foot in the dark."

"Come on, now," Melvin said. "We'll ride you folks back to town so you can see to your girlfriend's leg. What is it, a sprain?"

"We think so," Scott said, despite the fact that they hadn't discussed it.

Clara advised, "Well, you best get her to a hospital."

And Julie piped up to protest, "No need for that."

That was when Melvin smiled down on her, suddenly seeming like the sweetest old guy on the planet. "Come on, now," he said, "let me help ya to the truck."

Scott spoken up quickly, though, to say, "That's okay. I can take care of her." And with that, he rose to his feet, still cradling her snugly in his arms.

She leaned her face into his strong, warm chest as he maneuvered them up the aisle, and she clutched at his neck even tighter now. She wanted to hold onto him forever. She wanted to be what Melvin had called her: Scott's girlfriend. And she wanted him to do just what he'd said—take care of her.

Scott followed Melvin and Clara's flashlight up the hill with Julie in his grasp. The rain had stopped and she leaned her head back to gaze at the sky. The moon shone overhead again, even brighter than before, as if freshened by the rain, and the sky had turned a deep midnight blue.

Looking ahead, however, she noticed that Melvin and Clara, even at their advanced age, scaled the hill much easier than Scott.

"Am I too heavy?" she whispered.

He shook his head. "No, honey, you're just right."

And her heart fluttered with all she felt for him, all she wanted to do with him. When her fright had subsided, her desire had returned—and sensations of want rippled over her skin, down through her body. She found herself running her fingers through his hair as he carried her.

"I want you," she whispered. She hadn't even thought about it—the words had just tumbled from her involuntarily, like fate, something meant to be. She didn't think she'd ever wanted anyone or anything more.

His eyes shone wide and deep on her beneath the

glow of the moon. "God, I want you, too," he whispered. "And as soon as we get out of here, back to civilization, where I can get you alone again, I'm gonna have you."

Julie parted her lips sensually, instinctually, in invitation. And his mouth brushed gently across hers, sending a soft jolt of electricity coursing through her veins. She drew in her breath, then kissed him again—and this time the kiss was stronger, their mouths struggling against each other like two hot, writhing bodies. She pulled back from him, her breath ragged.

"You kids okay back there?" Melvin shouted from above, his location marked by the beam of his flashlight.

Scott hesitated only slightly. "We're coming," he yelled. Then he lowered his voice for Julie. "I like Melvin, but he's got one hell of a bad sense of timing."

"I agree," she said with a giggle. Then she nuzzled against his neck, planting a tiny kiss below his ear.

She saw his heated little shiver before he smiled down at her. "Quit that now," he said. "Or I'll never get you to Melvin's truck in one piece."

"I can't wait for you to get me back out of it," she whispered, pleased when he let out a sexy little growl only she could hear, then leaned his head back, eyes half-shut with pleasure.

Julie had never experienced such an emotional release with a man. She'd never been so direct, so forward, so openly wanting. She'd never found a man who had made her feel so willing to share.

Her relationship with Patrick had been so fraught

with sexual pressures; nothing she'd ever given him had been enough. And only now did she begin to see that it never would have been.

But maybe with Scott it could be different. He loved the way she looked, even in a witch's costume. And he liked to do more than touch her—he talked to her and laughed with her and cared about how she felt, both inside and out. And it seemed as if he'd been almost as worried as her when they'd gotten separated in the dark. Unlike Patrick, Scott let her be who she wanted to be, who she really *was*.

Of course, she'd only known him for a matter of hours and first impressions could be deceiving, but she couldn't help feeling that this first meeting had gone way beyond the surface. They'd dealt with hardship together, made decisions, even faced imminent death—or so they'd thought. She couldn't push down the sense that she truly knew him somehow, and that he truly knew her, too.

She realized that she was smack dab in the middle of a night that would change her life forever.

For one thing, she knew she no longer needed, or even wanted, Patrick. And maybe all this time she'd just been hanging on to some idea of what she *wanted* him to be, wishing he would change—even if people seldom did. It could be easy to do that when someone had your heart and no one came along to show you something better.

And for another, she thought perhaps she had found

the man she *did* want—for today, for tomorrow, maybe for always. Scott was, this quickly, fulfilling the *something better* part of that equation, showing her what she'd been missing out on, and bringing out a side of her she'd never known. A fun side. A happy side. A flirty side. A sexual side. A brave side.

Lifting her hand to his chest, she felt the strong, pure beat of his heart. And despite the eerie dampness in the air and the dull ache that spread from her hip to her ankle, she felt as though she had never experienced a moment so perfect. She sighed with the enormous contentment that filled her.

Scott misread her expression, however, and peered down at her with concern. "Getting tired?"

She shook her head. "Just the opposite. Invigorated."

And this time he read her perfectly. "Well, I'm getting damn aroused," he said with a smile. Melvin's truck wasn't far away.

"I hope your bones are ready to be jumped," she whispered.

His sexy grin grew—but then his eyes narrowed with doubt. "You're making awfully bold promises for a woman with a bum leg."

"There are more important body parts," she offered gently as they stepped into the shafts of light that glowed from the front of Melvin's truck. Scott flashed a quiet, knowing smile as he carried her around to the door on the other side.

"Hop on up in here," Melvin said then. "Don't be

shy."

The truck was a small 1950's Ford. Clara sat in the middle of the old bench seat, pressed against Melvin's large body, leaving just enough room for one more person to squeeze in comfortably. "You don't mind ridin' your girlfriend on your lap, do ya?" Melvin asked.

"No, that's fine," Scott said.

"I didn't think so. Since she was settin' on your lap in the school bus even with all them empty seats to choose from." He finished with a laugh.

After which Clara smacked his thigh and offered up a, "Shush, old man."

Scott slowly maneuvered them both into the cramped seat, then slammed the door tight behind them, locking it so Julie could lean back against it safely.

His arms enveloped her, one circling her waist from behind, the other stretched across both her legs, his hand holding firmly to her thigh. Her left breast crushed softly against his chest, the connection with him bringing her nipples to life beneath the bra that suddenly seemed special not because of the ballet, but because Scott would soon see it—Scott would soon take it off of her. Her body was on fire for him. She looked into his eyes and let him see the flames there, the passion she no longer wanted to keep secret from him.

His response quickly rose beneath her, pushing into Julie's hip. Despite their companions, she suffered the incredible urge to turn and straddle him in the seat.

"So, you kids been together long?" Melvin asked

above the roar of the old truck's motor as it rumbled over a gravel path.

"No," Scott replied. "We just met tonight."

And when Julie drew her eyes from the windshield to cast him a wide-eyed look of reproach, Melvin just let out another of his good-natured laughs.

Even Clara smiled. Then patted Julie's knee. "Don't you worry none, hon. I think the reason Melvin asked is probably cuz you seem so comfy together. Somethin' like that don't usually happen all at once. But when it does," she added with a wink, "that might just mean it's worth hangin' on to."

Julie's face heated with what she suspected was a crimson blush, but she gave the woman a friendly smile anyway. And Scott smiled, too, but she couldn't bring herself to look directly into his eyes at that moment. She knew he wanted her madly, but she wasn't brave enough just yet to ponder for how long, and she didn't want him to be scared off by phrases like *worth hanging on to*. She wanted him to decide that for himself.

When the truck finally emerged onto a paved road, Scott gave Melvin directions back to the party. Julie thought it felt like a week had passed since they'd left it.

As they drove back to town, Clara took the liberty of examining Julie's sprained ankle, announcing it was swollen something fierce and also had a sizable bump. Meanwhile, Julie gazed out the window thinking how wonderful and safe it felt to be back among lights, and houses, and streets with yellow lines painted down the middle.

"You're gonna take her to an emergency room, ain't ya?" Clara asked Scott.

"No," Julie said quickly, but both of them ignored her.

"Do you think it's necessary?" Scott asked.

"That's a mighty nasty bump there. And it's always best to make sure with these things, get some X-rays and not take no chances. Never know when there's a broken bone in there needin' to be fixed."

"You best listen to Clara," Melvin instructed. "She spent thirty-five years in nursin'."

"Really?" Scott asked, seeming duly impressed. "Well then, if you say we should get X-rays, we'll get X-rays."

Julie started to protest again, but Scott covered her mouth with his hand. "Not a word, young lady."

"But—"

"Take a right here, Melvin," he said. Then lowly to Julie, "We're almost back to the party. Let's deal with it after we get out so these nice people can get on with their lives."

She couldn't argue with that logic, so she stayed silent. And hoped that Scott had agreed merely to quiet Clara's concerns. She'd never been to the hospital in her life and she wasn't about to go now just for a little bump on her ankle. Besides, she had much more important plans than going to the hospital. A certain skeleton's bones needed jumping.

"You can let us out here by my car," Scott said,

pointing out the window to a late model four-door that surprised Julie not so much with its luxury, but with its mature, low-key style. Yet she certainly didn't mind. A comfy back seat would be wonderful for the private party she waited to engage in. And he'd parked nearly a block from the party, which would make for plenty of privacy.

"You're headed straight to the emergency room from here, right?" Clara asked yet one more time.

"You better believe it," Scott promised her.

Just as when they'd gotten in the truck, he lowered Julie gently to the ground, carefully maneuvering her sore leg so that it didn't bang against the seat or the door.

"We can't thank you enough," he said, looking back into the truck. "You really saved us out there."

"Pshaw," Melvin said, waving a hand downward through the air. "I got a feelin' you'd a been fine."

"Well, you never know."

Melvin chuckled. "Reckon you're right. Daryl Dukes coulda got ya. Boo!" he said, letting his eyes go big and round.

They all laughed—despite that Julie had had enough scares for one night.

"You get that leg tended to now," Clara said in parting.

Julie, standing on one foot and leaning against Scott's car, nodded and waved. And Scott slammed the door on the old truck, then stepped back beside her. Both stayed quiet as they watched Melvin turn his truck around in a nearby cul-de-sac, the taillights soon fading into the distance.

"Nice people," Scott said.

"Very Brady, after all," Julie agreed.

"I might not go *that* far," Scott said. "Melvin struck me as more the Green Acres type. I've always wondered whatever happened to Mr. Haney. I think I know now."

Julie giggled.

"Listen," he said, turning to her and suddenly looking more serious, "I'm really sorry about what happened out there, about losing you in the dark."

"It's all right," she promised. "I'm the one who went running off into the night."

But he argued. "No, it's not. If not for me, you wouldn't have hurt your ankle."

"Yet if not for that," she pointed out softly, "I might never have asked you to kiss me."

He gazed down on her thoughtfully. "Oh, come on now," he whispered with a playful smile. "You would have eventually."

And she conceded with a flirtatious tilt of her head. "I guess you're right."

How good it felt to finally be alone with him. Julie's heart trembled in her chest. She felt so fresh, so new, even after the horrors they'd been through, even with the dirt that covered their clothes, even with the dull aching of her ankle below. She felt as if something in her had been reborn as she'd traveled those fields with Scott—and she wanted to show him the woman she'd become.

She reached down, still careful not to sink any weight

onto her throbbing ankle, and found the handle on the back door of his car. Clicking it gently open, she pushed it wide enough to lower herself onto the seat.

He gazed down at her beneath the soft glow of a streetlight overhead, eyes shimmering. "Leg hurting?"

"Some," she said. "Not much."

"Come on," he said. "Let me carry you around to the front seat. Unless you'd rather lie down in back," he added. "If it's hurting—"

"I want to lie down," she said, a sexy rasp in her voice she'd never heard before. "But not by myself. With you." She reached her hand up to him, letting hunger flash in her eyes.

"Julie," he said with a heavy sigh. "It's not that I wouldn't love to. You know that. But your leg."

She blinked. "What about it?"

"It needs to be tended to," he said, using Clara's words.

"No, it doesn't. It's fine. I promise. If it wasn't, would I feel this way now? Would I be feeling just like I did back on the bus. Don't you remember?" She dropped her voice to a sexy whisper. "I want you."

"I want you, too," he said, his tone unduly exasperated. "But I also want you *well*. Now, come on—we're going to the ER."

Huh. He didn't *sound* like someone who wanted her. He *sounded* like someone who was bossing her around, treating her like a little kid. He sounded like...Patrick.

Humiliation warmed Julie's face. She had actually

found the courage, the openness, to offer herself to a man this way—and he had actually turned her down? "You can't be serious," she finally sputtered.

"I am. Completely. What kind of heel would climb in that back seat with a woman in pain, a woman who needs to see a doctor? I want you, Julie—but I don't want you *that* bad."

She gasped, the way he'd spoken to her singeing her heart. She felt…dismissed.

Perhaps the connection between them had been imaginary? Perhaps he'd wanted a body, *any* body, when skulking about a party, or looking for fun in a haunted house. Perhaps he'd never really wanted *her*.

Or maybe…he'd gotten a better look at her now that they were back in town. She must look like hell by now. Perhaps with the aid of streetlights and headlights and houselights, he'd decided she wasn't as appealing as she'd been out in the dark nothingness of the countryside.

She reached up then, toward her face, suddenly remembering something she hadn't thought about in hours. Her mask. The little black velvet one. She touched two fingers to her right temple, then moved them toward her eye, aching to feel the velvet—that tiny bit of protection. But it was gone. Like the hat, she'd lost it somewhere along the way.

"You haven't had it on for hours," Scott said, peering down at her. "Not since the haunted house."

"Oh," she whispered. She felt naked. She'd managed to hide so little from him, and now that she suddenly felt at odds with him again, she realized she hadn't even been able to hide that one tiny piece of herself that had seemed to make such a difference when she'd entered the party earlier that night.

He could see her face. He could see the blatant lust in her eyes. He could see all of her. And she suddenly wasn't sure it had been wise to let him.

An urge re-invaded her body then, the same urge that had gripped her back in the field when he'd dipped his warm tongue between her breasts. She shivered at the memory, but the growing impulse to run away from him drowned the thick tinge of pleasure.

She rose from the back seat of the car, saying, "Excuse me," to Scott as she pushed him out of her way. Then, using the car for support, she moved awkwardly around it to the sidewalk.

"Where do you think *you're* going?" he asked, starting to follow her.

She parted from the car, gritting her teeth at the first unbearable step on her sore ankle. Not to mention those horrible blisters, and her aching toes. She hissed at the pain, hoping he hadn't heard. "I'm going to find Rhonda," she informed him, limping up the sidewalk toward the party.

"You're kidding," he said, catching up with her. "You can't even walk, Julie."

"That's funny," she replied, fighting to hide her agony, "since I seem to be walking, don't I?"

"Not very well," he pointed out. "Let me help you."

He slid his arm firmly around her waist, setting off a multitude of confusing sensations in her body. How warm he was. How sweet. How insensitive and bossy. What a pig. Did she love him or hate him? She couldn't decide.

But hate was easier. No risk involved. And how dare he confuse her this way? She just wanted to get away from him. To somewhere safe. And warm. Why, oh why, hadn't she just curled up with that good book tonight like she'd wanted to in the first place?

"Don't touch me!" she spewed at him, the words coming out angry and bitter. More ugly truth for him to see in her, but she didn't care now.

Hearing the venom in her voice, he jerked his hand away. "What did you say?" he shot back in disbelief.

"I said don't touch me," she replied, working to keep her voice even.

"Well, that's quite a change from a few minutes ago when you were begging me for sex," he said. "'Touch me', 'Don't touch me'. You're not making any sense."

"You're disgusting!" she snapped, limping ahead. How dare he remind her of what she'd wanted, of what he'd made her feel, of what she'd finally thought she could say to a man! "You're a filthy, disgusting pig!"

Scott stood on the sidewalk, eyes wide, mouth hanging open, apparently aghast and confused by her words. But she had no intention of explaining. She didn't owe him anything. She just wanted to get far, far away from him and forget she'd ever laid eyes on the guy in the skeleton suit.

That was when she realized the pain in her ankle had became excruciating. She had limped farther up the street as they'd argued and now each time she lowered her weight on her leg, it felt as if it would burst.

"You need to go to the hospital!" he said gruffly from behind her. But his voice came from farther away than before. Perhaps he was no longer following.

Julie slowly rounded a bend in the street, the party house finally coming into view. Seemed the party was still going on, but with an added attraction.

Flashing lights cast an eerie blue glow through the air. Four police cars had managed to squeeze their way into the yard. She saw a grim reaper being taken away in handcuffs. And Big Bird struggled with another police-man near the door, a flurry of yellow feathers flying in the darkness. She let herself sink to the sidewalk as she watched, her leg throbbing endlessly.

"Things must have gotten out of hand," Scott said, approaching from behind.

Just then a woman in a short black skirt and a lacy bra was dragged out onto the front stoop. She wore red high heels, black fishnet stockings that stopped just above the knee, and enough makeup for Julie to clearly see the outline of her lips from two houses away. "Is she supposed to be a hooker?" Julie mused.

"No," Scott said, "she's supposed to be a stripper. But she might have become a hooker by now."

She nodded below him, thinking maybe it *was* better

they'd left the party, even after all that had happened. "I'm glad I wasn't in there," she whispered.

"I'm glad you weren't either," he returned quietly.

They watched the action in silence as a few more monsters were herded from the house, along with Snow White, two rowdy dwarves, and the entire six-pack of beer she'd seen earlier. One can broke loose in the yard, but a quick-witted cop grabbed him before he got away, crushing the can when he tackled it.

"You're not going back in there?" Scott finally asked.

"No," she said below him.

"Come on then," he whispered.

She glanced up to see his eyes shining down on her, the glowing bones of one arm outstretched to help her stand. She accepted his hand and slowly rose to her feet.

That was when he hoisted her up over his shoulder, his arm locked firmly around her thighs as he trudged back down the sidewalk toward his car.

She couldn't believe it.

But on second thought, yes she could. The jerk had tricked her.

"You can't make me go to the hospital!" she cried, beating on his back with both fists. "You can't!"

"Wanna bet, Witchiepoo?" And just to make his point clear, he gave her a firm smack on the behind.

Chapter Nine

THE RECENT RAIN had left the road shiny and slick. The only colors she saw in the darkness ahead were the orange and red leaves swirling in the headlights of Scott's car.

"Know any jokes?" he asked her.

"What?" she snapped.

"I said do you know any jokes?"

She still couldn't believe he'd carried her down the street and shoved her into his car like an escaped prisoner. *And* swatted her behind! Who did he think he was anyway? "How can you possibly think about jokes at a time like this?"

"I personally think it's a pretty damn good time for a joke," he replied. "Geez, we need something to break the tension in here."

His brown eyes had been hopeful when he'd spoken, but Julie continued to stare indignantly out the windshield. She was being taken to the hospital against her will. She didn't want to hear any jokes.

"Okay," he said. "I've got one. Did you hear about

the dyslexic Agnostic?"

She glared at him.

"He wasn't sure if he believed there was a dog."

She continued to glare.

"Get it?" he asked with raised eyebrows. "Dog. God." He paused, waiting for a reply. "Dyslexic. Agnostic."

"I get it!"

Scott sighed and rolled his eyes. But she didn't care. She continued to direct her gaze out the window in silent protest.

"Okay," he said, "I've got another one. Knock, knock."

She lifted her chin in a small show of defiance and continued to ignore him.

"I said," he began slowly, "*Knock, knock.*"

Turning to scowl at him with narrowed eyes, she offered a sigh of disgust, and her voice came out quiet but decidedly cold. "Who's there?"

"Impatient cow."

She hesitated, thinking. What the hell could that mean? Would it turn out to be something embarrassing or dirty? Knowing Scott, the second option. She took a deep breath. "Impa-"

"Moo!"

She continued to glower at him, resuming her silence. Then she turned back to face the windshield.

"Man," he muttered, "tough room."

"You have no right," she suddenly spewed at him as the car careened around a bend in the road.

"I don't need to have a right," he responded without emotion.

"And you ran that stop sign back there, by the way."

"I did not."

"You didn't come to a complete stop. And you certainly didn't wait three seconds before proceeding."

"Who *are* you? The annoyance police?"

She harrumphed. "I just don't want to go to the hospital, that's all. And I don't like being forced."

"If you weren't so stubborn, I wouldn't have to force you, would I?"

"And if you would mind your own business, I wouldn't have to be so stubborn. And would you mind slowing down, Speed Racer?"

He accelerated slightly. And her blood boiled.

"If I'm Speed Racer," he said, "that would make you Trixie. But that can't be right. Because Trixie was much nicer."

She just rolled her eyes and muttered, "Trixie was a slut."

He turned to her with a disbelieving look. "What?"

"You heard me. She was a slut. You know she and Speed were doing it."

Her companion's mouth spread into an amused grin. "And you deduced this as a little kid? Sounds like you were sexually advanced."

"I just mean that she was one of those Barbie doll cartoon characters. Her body was way more grown-up than it needed to be to entertain small children."

"Ah. So you *assume* the animated Trixie was a slut merely because of how she was drawn."

"Actually," Julie explained, thinking back, "I think my older brother put that in my head. He had a thing for Trixie."

Scott nodded knowingly. "I was a Judy Jetson man myself."

"Figures," she groused. "You seem like the type to go after an innocent high school girl."

He cleared his throat. "Well, at the time, she was actually a much older woman. I was younger than Elroy at the time. And speaking of older women, that reminds me of another one. Josie. Of Josie and the Pussycats fame. I was even more a Josie man than a Judy man. Very hot."

"Oh yeah?"

"Redheads are sexy," he offered.

"Oh," she said indignantly. "Well, thanks a whole hell of a lot."

She felt his irritating grin before she saw it. "This is entertaining," he mumbled.

"What is?" she stormed at his taunting eyes.

"You, Witchiepoo. You're jealous of a cartoon character."

Julie peered at Scott for a moment, then turned back to face the road, trying to blot his gloating smile from her mind. God, he was right. It had been a long night. Rather than confirm the accusation, though, she said, "You are absolutely nuts."

"Me? I'm not the one who thinks I'm in competition

with an animated girl in a leopard suit. Which, by the way," he added, "would be a great costume. That's what you should dress up as next year."

"I can't—I'm not a redhead," she sniped. "Besides which, I can guarantee you that I won't be dressing up as *anything* next year." The surreal quality of the night had suddenly hit Julie full force: A haggard witch and a tattered skeleton driving down the road together looking like they'd just made a road trip to hell.

"I mean, really," she went on, "who ever heard of such a thing? Grown people dressing up and parading around, having a contest to see who can look the most absurd. Halloween is for kids. Look at me. And look at you. We both look ridiculous."

Scott's eyes narrowed and his voice grew suddenly serious. "Thanks a lot."

She tossed him a sideways glance. "What? Mr. I'm-Always-The-Cool-Guy is mad at me now?"

"Not mad," he said. "But I wouldn't mind if you kept your insults to yourself."

And her own anger began to slowly rise even higher at his belittling tone. How dare *he* act mad at *her*. She'd merely stated an obvious truth, for heaven's sake. And how dare he force her to go someplace she didn't want to go! She surged ahead, spewing out everything on her mind.

"That's another thing," she began. "I realize you think you're very clever for getting me to lighten up and talk TV with you, but I'm no less upset than I was before. In fact, it infuriates me that you think you have some hold on me, that you think you can control me. I don't even know you and here you are, physically dragging me off to someplace I don't want to go. So no matter how cute and funny you think you are, you're not."

As a heavy silence filled the car then, she could have sworn she heard her own heartbeat.

"So after all this," Scott said quietly, "you'd rather be enemies than friends?"

Despite everything, the question hit her harder than she might have expected. It sounded like such a final thing.

And still, inside she steamed. She felt as though she'd been manipulated by him the entire night. And just like parties and haunted houses, she had an irrational fear of hospitals and thought the decision to go there should be hers, not his. It simply wasn't fair. So she finally replied, "As long as you insist on forcing me to go to the hospital, yes."

"You know what?" he said, turning toward her.

"Keep your eyes on the road, please."

He ignored her command. "I should have paid attention to you earlier."

"When?"

"When I first met you. When I first opened the door at the party and saw you standing there with your little Witchiepoo mask and your little Vroom-broom. You were sending out all the signals."

"What signals?"

"The signals that said 'leave me alone'. The signals that said 'get the hell away from me'. But did I listen? No. I forged ahead. I talked. I flirted. I tried to bring you out of your shell and make you have a little fun. But I should have done just what you wanted and left you alone. Then I wouldn't be in the position of having to force an indignant woman with a potentially serious injury to go to the emergency room. And I wouldn't be in the position of being insulted by that same indignant woman just because I choose to have a little fun on Halloween.

"But I screwed up," he pressed on. "And here we are, both paying for it. So why don't you do us both a favor and just sit there and be quiet. You had the bad luck of getting stuck in a haunted house with me and spraining your ankle with me. And like it or not, you're going to the hospital. It'll be over soon. And after that you can hate me forever and chalk this up as the worst night of your life."

Julie was speechless. She supposed that had been his intention, but she'd never have imagined he could sound so cold. A mixture of anger and humiliation crept up her face in an unpleasant heat. She stared out the passenger window, actually trembling with something near to rage.

Okay, so maybe she'd taken her ER protests a little too far. But it had gone beyond a fear of hospitals. It was simply a matter of principle now. She didn't like having a man tell her what to do. Again, it was so very Patrick.

Wear this. Walk like that. Go here, and then there. It was a very different situation, yet it still pinched a nerve inside her. She'd never been able to stand up to Patrick, but she would certainly stand up to Scott—he couldn't boss her around.

What really bothered her, though, when she thought about it, was that apparently Scott *could* boss her around. He was taking her to the hospital and it was simply beyond her ability to halt the stupid trip. He'd just told her to be quiet and there she sat, silent as a mouse. His success added to her internal outrage.

The car continued to move over the glistening road, growing closer to the dreaded hospital, and Julie felt helpless. But as they drove up the slick lane that led to the emergency room door, something about the place seemed even more eerie than she'd expected.

A bright glow emanated from the entrance, the misty air subtly fusing the white light with the gleaming red letters above. The spooky glow was the only semblance of light that could be seen from the car, the words *Emergency Room* hovering in the damp night air like a threat. Julie suddenly imagined going inside those doors and never being allowed to leave.

Of course, she knew that it was probably her imagination, as so much had been tonight already. The illusion that the chainsaw in the haunted house had been real. The illusion that Melvin was a serial killer. The illusion that she'd been falling in love with Scott. Right now she was so angry at him that she could barely even look at him, let alone remember the warmth she'd felt for him a mere hour earlier.

"The lights look weird," Scott said, squinting toward the entrance.

She didn't respond, but felt reassured. At least she wasn't imagining things anymore.

"Kinda spooky," he added in a playful way that was probably meant to scare her.

And if scaring her was his intention, it worked. "I don't like it here," she said. "Take me home."

"Forget it," he replied, screeching the car up to the curb just outside the dark entrance. He yanked the keys from the ignition, then got out, slamming the door behind him. The glowing bones circled the car quickly and her stomach grew thick with the familiar nervousness that had haunted her all night.

On impulse, she reached over and locked her door.

Outside the window, he rolled his eyes at her immaturity and calmly pushed a button on his keychain that reversed the action. Then he opened her door and, before she could utter a word, reached in and scooped her into his arms.

An instant heat surged through her veins at being so close to him again. Like in the woods. Like in the bus. She hated it. And she loved it. Her eyes met his only fleetingly before she glanced down. She knew he'd seen the horrible flash of desire within them, but she chose to silently deny it anyway, quickly replacing it with a scowl. Still, it did nothing to decrease the ticklish feeling in her panties, and inside she ached over all the conflicting emotions that consumed her. She wondered if it was too late to make up with him, to pretend they hadn't argued, to start over somehow.

He maneuvered them into a revolving door that, thankfully, contained wide enough compartments that her leg didn't bump against the glass.

Then he whisked her into the room, suddenly and excruciatingly bright, the overhead lights nearly blinding. The intense artificial light was beyond shocking after having spent so much time in the darkness with him. If she'd looked bad beneath the dim streetlights back at the party, how must she look now? The place hustled and bustled like any other emergency room, too busy and jarring to nurture ideas of forgiveness, and her fleeting hopes of reconciliation fizzled as he carried her to the admissions desk.

The desk was occupied by a woman dressed as Cinderella—she wore a flowing blue evening gown and long satin gloves, and her desk was adorned with a pair of clear pumps sporting three-inch heels. "Can I help you?" the chiffon-clad woman asked as Julie and Scott drew near.

"Sprained ankle," Scott said, none-too-gently depositing Julie in a chair across from the desk. "Unwilling patient," he further informed her. "If not for the inability to walk, I think she'd make a run for it."

"Don't try it," Cinderella warned her with a smile.

But Julie didn't respond. She was in no mood to

make friends. All she could think about was the incredible brightness of the room, how the light shone down on her dirty dress and disheveled hair, how it seemed to glare on all the night's events, making them reality. She glanced up at Scott, noticing that he suffered an equal state of disarray.

Cinderella smiled sympathetically. "Look," she said to Julie, "no one wants to be here. But if you're hurt, it's best."

Yet again Julie refrained from replying. She knew Cinderella had good intentions, but she was sick of the whole world ganging up on her about this. She wanted to crawl into a hole.

"Name?" Cinderella began keying Julie's vital information into a computer, the screen casting a gentle green glow over her blue dress. "Date of birth?"

Julie answered questions as Scott excused himself to go to the restroom. When Cinderella finished, she said, "Somebody will be with you in a minute."

Scott returned almost as quickly as he'd left. "So," he said to Cinderella, "you're what? The prom queen?"

She issued a disgusted yet playful sigh, grabbing up one of the clear shoes by the heel and tapping its toe against the desk. "This tip you off any, Einstein?" she asked with a smile.

Julie wondered if Scott would act insulted, but instead he just laughed. How she envied his easy-going demeanor. Easy-going, it seemed, until it came to her. He took the woman's shoe from her hand and studied it.

"This is plastic," he said.

"Practicality," Cinderella explained dryly. "This *is* a hospital, you know."

"I still say you look like my prom date."

Just then, a soft voice called Julie's name and both Julie and Scott looked up, searching for the voice's source.

"To your right," Cinderella said, pointing.

And Scott leaned down to once again lift Julie into his arms. Into his warmth.

"Save a slow dance for me, Cindy," he said over his shoulder as he carried Julie down the hall.

Her stomach quivered and she prayed Scott couldn't see how jealous she was of his flirtations—flirtations that had for a while been reserved only for her.

And what on earth gave him the courage to flirt now, anyway? Didn't the man remember he was wearing a bizarre-looking skeleton suit? And that his face was streaked with black and white makeup?

But Scott wasn't like her, she remembered—he didn't assume people would respond to him merely on the merits of his appearance.

And then she began to recall a further truth about Scott, this one not so wholesome or flattering. He was a *huge* flirt—it seemed inherent in his personality. And he liked it that way. He wanted no commitments. No ties.

Just thank God she hadn't slept with him and gotten attached. Thank God things had stopped before his lies about caring for her had whisked her into total oblivion.

Thank God fate had intervened and stopped her from making a gigantic mistake.

"This way," Julie heard the same silky voice summon them.

Scott carried her, following the voice, until he entered a small room and lay her gently on a cold examination table. Everything felt crisp and looked sterile, reigniting her fear. The long narrow fluorescent bulb overhead seemed too bright, like all the lights in this horrible place, emphasizing the stark, cold feel of the room.

Everything was so white—white walls, white cabinets, white tables. The only things not in white were made of a shiny stainless steel that chilled her on sight. The fear in her stomach snaked its way through her entire body until she trembled all over, and she hugged herself, trying to still her shivers and ward off the cold.

But she nearly forgot all of that when she caught sight of the silky voice from before: a blond in a white halter dress.

"Marilyn Monroe?" Scott asked.

Marilyn smiled in response.

"*Seven Year Itch*," he added, connecting her dress and the movie with his typical easy smile.

"That's right," she replied breathily.

Scott nodded, and Julie fumed inside. But she couldn't figure out why. She'd already reminded herself what a cad he was, after all, so why did it matter anymore? Why on earth should she care if he wanted to flirt with every costumed female in the building.

"The doctor will be right with you," Marilyn said in her whispery way, then disappeared through the door.

"Great costume, huh?" Scott asked.

And Julie rolled her eyes. "If you like that sort of thing."

"What sort of thing?"

"That...sex-appeally sort of thing."

"I guess you weren't using that with *your* costume, right?"

Julie didn't reply, just let her returning ire build.

"Jealous?" he asked playfully.

"No, I'm not jealous," she snapped. "I'm angry and I'm tired and my leg aches and I want to go home. But I'm certainly not jealous."

Scott walked around the table, his eyes never leaving her. She could feel his surveying stare, and the longer it lasted, the more unnerving it became.

She continued to hold her own gaze on the ceiling. Where it was safe. Where her anger wouldn't waver or collapse. Where no emotion would threaten to leak free.

When he finally spoke, his voice came slow and deep and laced with a severe edge. "You know what your problem is?"

She didn't respond.

"You take things too damn seriously," he said. "Costume parties, haunted houses, X-rays. You *certainly* take other women too seriously." He shook his head, as if in disbelief. "Hell, you even take your own *dress* too seriously."

She slowly pulled her gaze from the white ceiling tiles to meet his eyes. Still the same deep brown as before. But cold now.

"I should have figured this out before," he told her.

"Figured what out?" she whispered through the chilled air.

"You. I thought you were warming up to me. Getting softer. Nicer. Sweeter. Out there in the field, in the bus. I guess I thought I was getting to know you, and getting to like you. A lot. But as soon as we got back to town, you reverted to your cold prim-and-proper routine. This is the *real* you. And that part of you I saw out in the darkness tonight—I guess that was just imaginary."

"What are you talking about?" she asked him, her voice still a whisper.

"I've heard that for some women danger and desperation are a big turn-on," he said. "I've never actually experienced it before, but now I see just how it works."

"*What?*" Julie sat up on the table, aghast at his suggestion.

"Out there in the darkness," Scott began, "in the middle of nowhere, when you were afraid, you wanted me so bad you couldn't think straight. But now that that's all over and you're safe again, you're the same indignant Witchiepoo I met at the party. You never really wanted me at all, did you? Not the right way. Not the way *I* wanted *you*."

His words left her lightheaded. "That's not true, Scott. I—"

"Hello there," came a new voice.

And Julie turned her head to see a doctor in a white coat—he stood in the doorway removing a pair of bloody rubber gloves.

Her mind flashed on the messy hospital scene back at the haunted house—doctors and knives and blood and screaming, patients with missing arms and legs. Feeling trapped between Scott's accusing words and the fear that had finally reached a point of overflow, she felt her body begin to crumble. And then she fainted.

Chapter Ten

SCOTT STOOD OVER Julie while the doctor turned her foot this way and that on the table, taking X-rays. But his eyes weren't on her ankle. He watched her face. She looked so peaceful sleeping there. Much more at ease than he'd seen her before and it surprised him. How pretty she looked, prettier than he'd realized. Even with that little smudge of dirt on her cheek.

He reached down to wipe at it with two fingers, using his other hand to hold back the loose material he'd ripped away from his hand earlier to touch her, skin to skin. He winced at the memory. Then, despite himself, he let his fingertips linger softly on her cheek.

He swallowed, remembering the last things he'd said to her before she'd passed out. Harsh words. And he wasn't sure if they were true or not, but they'd felt true when he'd said them.

The way she'd turned on him so suddenly when Melvin and Clara had dropped them at his car had hurt, damn it. Just because he'd wanted to make sure her leg was all right. Just because he wanted to do the right thing for her.

He assumed it was over now—whatever they had or hadn't shared out there in the darkness. Coming back to real life had changed the magic of the night, the magic of having only each other out there in the woods.

He assumed she would wake up and yell at him some more.

And then he would take her out to the car and she would yell at him some more.

And then he'd take her home and she would yell at him some more.

And then he'd never see her again.

That last thought was a sobering one. It sent a sharp, familiar pain soaring through his chest, much like what he'd felt when they'd been separated in the woods.

But he pushed it aside. It was useless, after all. A little pain never changed anything.

Still, he reached down to softly touch her face again.

EXHAUSTION ECHOED THROUGH every bone in Julie's body. With effort, she slowly eased her eyes open.

Two blurry figures hovered above her, growing clearer as the seconds passed by. To her left stood a doctor wielding noxious smelling salts. To her right, the skeleton who had made her life both bliss and torture over the past hours.

The full power of the smelling salts assaulted her nose. "Get those things away from me," she muttered.

And above her Scott said, "Ah, now there's the Witchiepoo I've come to know."

"We took the X-rays of your ankle while you were...asleep," the doctor announced. "Your friend thought that might be the best way."

Scott and the doctor exchanged a knowing glance and Julie switched her scowl from the doctor to Scott.

"Your ankle will be fine," the doctor went on. "It's a nasty twist, but nothing's broken. Now I want you to go home, get some sleep, and keep this leg elevated. I'm going to give you something for the pain to help you sleep tonight, but after that you're on your own. And I expect you to wake up feeling much better. When you get up tomorrow I want you to walk on it, carefully, and within a day or two it should be back to normal."

With that, the doctor reached into a white cabinet and extracted a small packet that struck Julie as looking like it would contain a miniature condom. He tore it open to produce two pills, which he placed in Julie's palm—as Marilyn Monroe entered the room, as if on cue, with a cup of water. Julie swallowed the pills with a gulp from the cup, then lay back on the table to rest.

"You're all set," the doctor said.

Julie still didn't reply, though. Just too tired. From everything.

"Would you like a wheelchair?" he asked Scott.

But Scott shook his head. "Not necessary." Then the doctor vacated the room, Marilyn and her fake mole clicking out on her heels behind him.

Julie rose to a sitting position, then slowly ⸏ legs over the edge of the table, her emotions dro a strange lethargy. Could the pills have taken ef quickly? Or maybe plain old-fashioned exhausti finally set in, ravaging her mind now that it had f with her body.

Either way, she didn't have the energy to yell at for putting her through just to find out what ⸏ already known—her ankle would be fine. And she di even have the energy to be mad at him for the horr things he'd been saying to her when she'd passed o She didn't have any energy at all. She just wanted to ⸏ to sleep.

As Scott wordlessly picked Julie up, she let her head rest against his strong shoulder. How easy it would be just to sleep there. Damn it, why did he still have to feel so good, so warm, so safe?

Another illusion, though. There was nothing safe about him.

And still, when he placed her in the car, it almost came as a shock to have his arms abandon her. She missed his nearness immediately.

"Do you want me to take you to your boyfriend's place?" Scott asked as he drove away from the hospital.

"No," she whispered quickly.

"Why not?" he asked. "You shouldn't be alone. You're supposed to stay off that until you get some rest, remember? You need someone to take care of you for a little while."

"He's, he's…got to get up early tomorrow," she sputtered, "and God only knows how late it is. So I'd rather not…you know…wake him."

"Won't he be worried? Don't you want to let him know you're okay?"

"Look," she said, more tired than angry, "we're engaged, not married. He doesn't have to know every single thing I do."

"Okay, okay, whatever you say," Scott told her. "I guess you wouldn't exactly want him to know about some of the stuff that happened tonight anyway, would you?" He sighed, but didn't wait for an answer. "You wanna come home with me then?"

Julie slowly turned her head to glare at him—and Scott merely shook his head as if she were an insolent child. She didn't think she'd ever met a more infuriating man in her life.

"I wasn't inviting you over for any big sexual extravaganza," he told her. "I meant in case you needed help getting around or something. In case you needed anything while you slept. For God's sake, when are you gonna figure out I'm just trying to help you?"

"Take me to Rhonda's," she instructed him. It was the only place she could think of that would feel comfortable. No pressure. No emotions. Just the sleep she craved.

"You want to go to Rhonda's?" he snapped. "Fine then—I'll take you to Rhonda's. Where does she live?"

"Glenbriar Apartments. Do you know them?"

"Yep," he said, voice stiff, eyes peering staunchly out over the darkened road.

The rest of the ride remained silent. And Julie couldn't think straight, about right or wrong, smart or stupid, what to do next.

Sleep. That was all she wanted. The pain pills were beginning to dull the ache in her ankle, beginning to drive reality away.

All she wanted was to finally get this horrible night over with. To get her life back to normal. Antiques. Candy apples. How much simpler. Who needed fun and excitement from a man in a skeleton suit? No. It was easier to exist alone. No risk. No worry. Just day-to-day life. Day…to day…to day.

When they arrived at the Glenbriar Apartments and she pointed out Rhonda's building, Scott parked the car, then hopped out and came around to her side.

And an unexpected tremble passed through her as he opened her door. Because she remembered what was coming. He would pick her up. Hold her close against him. Make her heart beat double time.

As anticipated, he handily whisked her into his arms, carrying her into Rhonda's building like crossing a honeymoon threshold. "Second door on the left," Julie whispered softly near his ear.

Her arms clutched at his neck almost involuntarily. How solid and strong his body still felt to her, even in the lethargy of a pain pill that had taken her very near to sleep. Again, she imagined sleeping right where she was.

In his arms.

She was jolted from her comfort, though, when Scott gently set her upright on the floor outside Rhonda's apartment. She opened her eyes, her arms still circling his neck, his hands still resting softly at her waist. He gazed down at her with those deep chocolate eyes, but she couldn't read them now. Everything had become too cloudy.

"Look," he said, his arms still around her, "about tonight, about everything—I'm sorry things got so…weird."

"Forget it," she said softly. Then, despite herself, "Thanks for making me go to the hospital. I guess you were right. It could have been broken or something." She couldn't believe her own words.

"The things I said at the hospital, Julie," he began, "right before you passed out. I didn't mean them."

She'd almost succeeded in pushing those words from her mind, and she didn't like being reminded. "Yes," she said gently, "you did."

He sighed. "Okay, I kind of did, but you were making me mad. I wanted you to be the way you were out in the fields. I was…disappointed, I guess."

She wondered vaguely if he meant he'd wanted her to be dying to have sex. But no, that was exactly how she *had* felt even after they'd *left* the fields. So he must have meant he wanted her to be some *other* way. But she was too tired, too spent, to think about it very hard—she couldn't even find the words to ask. So she merely stood there looking forlornly into his pretty eyes.

"I'm probably not your type anyway," he went on. "And even if I was, you're engaged."

"True," she whispered, her chest tightening with the absurd lie. "And besides, we both know how you feel about commitment."

"It's great for some people," he said. "Just not for me."

Julie nodded, remembering her first impression of him. Pushy. Suggestive. Rude. A born womanizer. Despite the soft, caring parts she'd discovered in him, she'd actually been right about him from the beginning. She swallowed hard in the face of the reality.

When he drew his arms away, she felt immediately empty without them around her. She let her own arms drop to her side as she leaned back against Rhonda's door, struggling to put most of her weight on her good ankle as he reached around her to press the doorbell twice.

He turned to go then, padding quietly up the hall, and she looked after him. *Not even a goodbye?*

When he reached the door, though, he stopped and looked back. "I sincerely hope you're happy, Witchie-poo," he said. But she could tell from the way he said it—he knew she wasn't. "Take care of that ankle."

"All right." Only she'd said it so quietly that he hadn't even heard. He had already disappeared out the door, his bones moving through the darkness until they were gone. She heard his car door slam, then listened until it pulled away. He had just disappeared from her life.

She sighed, then turned to begin banging on Rhonda's door with what little energy she had left.

"I'm coming, I'm coming," she heard her friend say from within until finally, the door flung open. Rhonda stood before her wearing a short, slinky robe, a pair of red horns still protruding from her tousled hair.

"Jules!" she said, throwing her arms around her. "I was worried sick."

"Ow, watch it," Julie replied. "I have a sprained ankle and any sudden jolt shoots pain directly to my foot."

Rhonda looked down. "How'd you sprain your ankle?" Then she looked back up. "And where's my hat? And my mask?" Her eyes moved down again. "And what kind of hell did you put this dress through?"

"Your hat and mask are long gone," Julie said, pushing past Rhonda. "Beyond that, I don't feel much like explaining. I just need to get some sleep."

"Try to be quiet," Rhonda warned as Julie entered the apartment.

"Why?"

"I have company," Rhonda tittered.

And Julie raised her eyebrows in silent question.

"There's a vampire asleep in my bed," she explained.

Julie sighed. "Yeah, I can see now just how worried you were," she said with what little venom she could muster.

Rhonda frowned. "He wanted to comfort me." Then

she giggled. "And he keeps saying how he vants to suck my—"

"Stop, I don't want to know," Julie said, weakly throwing up a hand in protest. "Nor do I want to know why you're still wearing those horns."

Rhonda smiled wickedly. "They don't call me the kinky devil for nothin'."

Julie just rolled her eyes and sank onto the couch.

"Hey, and speaking of that," Rhonda said, "where's Skeleton Dude? That *is* who you've been with all this time, isn't it?"

She just kept it simple. "He dropped me off here and he's on his way home, I guess."

"You should have invited him in."

"Rhonda, all I want to do is sleep. Now, would you mind getting me some pillows and a blanket and helping me prop up this leg?"

Rhonda replied by planting her hands on her hips. "You screwed up, didn't you?"

But Julie ignored the accusation and just let her head sink back against the soft fabric of the sofa.

"You let him get away," her friend went on. "You had a perfectly great guy in your grasp and you lost him."

"May I have my pillows?"

Rhonda cast her a look of severe disappointment before padding to a nearby closet. Then she quickly pulled out pillows and blankets and went about the work of moving around Julie to fix the couch for sleep. "I can't believe you blew this," she said, stacking the pillows at one end. "I can't believe you let that great guy get away. Or should I say *drove* him away. Because I know you too well. He wasn't Patrick, right? He treated you too nice. He made you have too much fun. Am I right?"

"Look," Julie said, slowly lifting her sore leg onto the pile of pillows, "you don't know the guy, all right? He's not always so nice and so fun."

"If he's not, I'm sure it's your fault," Rhonda said matter-of-factly as she covered her with a blanket.

Another exhausted sigh snuck out. "Rhonda, just go back to your vampire and I'll talk to you in the morning. Okay? Please."

"It *is* the morning."

"Huh?"

"It's after five. It'll be light soon."

Julie sighed. "Then I need sleep worse than I thought. Go back to bed and leave me alone."

Rhonda gazed on her with rank disapproval again, then finally flipped off the light and disappeared down the hall, her horns still glittering in the darkness.

Finally, rest. She lay there, begging sleep to find her and knowing it wouldn't take long. But it didn't come before a jarring memory invaded her tired mind.

Scott, holding her, kissing her. The horrible, beautiful, needful way she had wanted him. It had been so far beyond her control. It had been beyond anything she'd ever felt. How had she succeeded in pushing that away?

And then a bitter truth seeped slowly into her mind. Alone in the dark, quiet room she could no longer deny it.

Scott had been right. She took things too seriously. It was a leftover result of her relationship with Patrick.

She knew she needed to change that about herself. And she even knew she *wanted* to change it. She wanted to have fun as much as anyone else did.

The challenge came in actually permitting herself to feel it, in actually recognizing that she could have fun if she only let her guard down.

She sighed, thinking of Scott. Sex with him could have been wild and tame at the same time, prurient and pure all in one. He would have been just the guy to help her get over those silly hang-ups and live for a change. He could have been the perfect man.

Rhonda had hit the nail on the head—Julie had screwed up and let him get away.

She wished everything was different. She wished they'd made love in the field. And on the bus. And in his car. Over and over again. She wished his strong arms were wrapped around her right now.

She shut her eyes tight, trying to clench back the tears, but they came anyway. She felt them rolling down her cheeks until she finally slipped into sleep.

STANDING BEFORE HIS bathroom mirror, Scott gazed for a moment at the smeared mess his face had become, then he ran a warm, wet wash cloth over his skin, removing what remained of his skeleton makeup.

Oddly, it felt strange. To be himself again. The way he was every other day of his life. He wondered if Julie had shed the witch's dress yet and turned back into an antique dealer.

He wondered, too, how things might have been different if they'd met like *this*, instead of like *that*. But he supposed he would never know, and that he probably wasn't meant to.

He cast off his skeleton suit, once a work of costume art, now not much more than a dirty, tattered piece of cloth painted with glowing bones. He let it drop in a heap, then stepped into a warm shower.

It felt refreshing, almost renewing, to wash it all away. The dirt and grime, the bits of dried blood on his forehead. The memories of Julie in his arms.

Okay, those didn't wash away so easily. But he turned the water on harder, hoping to drown his frustrations.

Once out of the shower, he pulled on a pair of gym shorts, then walked out into the living room where his mother had fallen asleep in the reclining chair waiting up for him all night.

"Sorry, mom," he said, bending to kiss her on the cheek.

"You've already said that, Scott," she told him. "It's all right."

"Still, I know how you worry."

His mother shook her head. "You've been a big boy for a long time now. I know you can take care of yourself."

"Why didn't you go to bed?" he asked her. "I made up the spare bedroom with fresh sheets and everything."

"Maybe I *like* waiting up for you," she said, smiling up at him with tired eyes. "Old habits die hard."

After he said goodnight to his mother, he stole quietly into the room next to his own. He stood watching silently, the moon still shining as it had through much of the night, casting a pale light through the window over the child tucked beneath racecar bedsheets. Then he crept over and bent to kiss the cheek of his six-year-old son.

Chapter Eleven

———

JULIE LET THE towel drop to the floor behind her. She slipped into fresh panties and a clean bra, then a loose pair of blue jeans and a big, oversized sweatshirt. How wonderful to be in clean, comfortable clothes! The shower she'd just taken had felt like a gift that had washed away everything bad.

When she stooped to retrieve the towel, careful not to put too much pressure on her ankle, her eyes fell on the black dress that lay in a heap next to her bed. How strange it had felt to unzip it and let it fall away from her body. Almost like a layer of her skin, a part of herself, had disappeared. Just the same, taking off the dress had been liberating. It was good to get back to normal.

But, she thought, still eyeing the dress, being sexy hadn't really been so awful either.

She plucked it up, along with the towel, and tossed them both in the clothes hamper. And hoped she would be able to forget. His eyes. His touch. Everything.

Pulling on a pair of socks, she padded softly into the kitchen and found a can of chicken soup in the pantry.

The weather outside was gray—maybe more rain was blowing in—and it seemed like a good day for a cozy cup of soup.

Rhonda had driven her home almost an hour ago, but it was already two in the afternoon. Seemed impossible that it could be that late—but she tried not to concentrate on all the time she felt she'd lost as she laid out mental plans for the rest of the day.

First, she would take her soup to the living room and curl up with her favorite throw and that same bestseller she'd missed last night. Then, in a few hours, when it got dark, trick-or-treating would begin and the kids would start coming for their candy apples.

And she would feel like her old self again, Julie the antique dealer, Julie the dispenser of old-fashioned homemade treats.

All would be well again. And it would be about time.

She stirred the soup and when it was hot, turned off the burner and poured a steaming mug for herself. Then she moved to her favorite reading spot next to the hearth. She settled on the couch, gingerly pulling her legs up beneath her. The doctor had been right—her ankle felt much better today. Almost normal. Almost like last night hadn't even happened. Almost.

She blew on her soup, then took a hot sip, letting it warm her. Then she opened her book and slipped out the bookmark, ready to read.

She hadn't made it through three pages, though, when the phone rang. She glanced up in irritation, then quickly slid her bookmark in place and rose to answer. She tried not to be too annoyed, figuring it was probably Rhonda calling to check up on her and make sure her ankle was still doing okay.

"Hello?"

"Julie, honey. Hi."

She froze in place, then let her back slide down the wall, her body sinking gently to the carpet. That voice. So smooth and cocky, so intoxicating in its very tone. She closed her eyes. "Patrick," she said.

"Hey princess, how you doing?"

"I'm fine," she said, too tired to think of anything clever or cutting. "How are you?"

He didn't answer right away, letting just the right length of time lapse to achieve the proper effect. "Not very good, angel."

What on earth was he calling her for? And why now, when she thought she'd finally gotten over him? "What's wrong?" she asked, vaguely curious if he could hear the sheer exhaustion in her voice.

Patrick sighed. "I made a big mistake, honey."

"Oh?" So that's what he was calling for. She could hear it coming.

"Baby, leaving you was the biggest mistake of my life."

"Did she dump you, Patrick?"

He was quiet. "Julie," he said, "this isn't about her. It's about you. And me, baby. The way things were. I want you back, angel. Forever."

Julie swallowed. She knew he was a jerk, but despite herself, that sexy voice had always been enough to bury her. It would have been so nice if the words were true, and once upon a time, in the not very distant past, she would have been tempted to believe him.

Yet even as a hint of a familiar old sensation passed through her body, something in her felt different than ever before. Maybe she felt prettier, or sexier. On the inside.

But she didn't want to be sexy for Patrick. He didn't understand sex; he didn't understand the intangible beauty in it—with him sex stayed physical. *I love you* meant *I want your body*. There was nothing else with him. Being with Scott, even for only a night, had made her understand so much about herself, so much that Patrick had abused and messed up. And she knew in that moment that she didn't want him anymore. Not at all. And if she felt prettier, or sexier, well then, she must want to be that way for—

"Did you hear me, baby?" he finally asked when she didn't respond. "I want you back."

"Listen, Patrick," she said, "I'm not feeling well so I'm going to get off the phone and lie down a while. Okay?"

"Why don't I come over and lie down *with* you?"

Typical Patrick response. "No thanks."

"I'll make it all better, angel. Whatever's wrong, I'll take it all away." More typical Patrick.

"I don't think so."

Her gruffness seemed to quiet him for a moment, or at least slow him down. "Don't be that way, baby. I love you."

"No, Patrick," Julie said, "you don't. You don't love anybody but yourself. And how dare you call me up after four months with someone else and invite yourself into my bed."

"Julie, sweetheart, listen to me. Can't we just kiss and make up? Put this behind us?"

Julie took a deep breath, and when she spoke, the words came out smooth and steady and strong. "I've already done that, Patrick. I've already put all this behind me."

"What do you mean?"

"I've moved on," she said. "And I suggest you do the same."

"Julie—"

"Don't call me again, Patrick."

She gently set down the receiver, quietly cutting off the connection. She thought proudly of the dial tone in his ear. Then she took the phone back off the hook, just in case he decided to ignore her last request.

She remained sitting on the floor a minute, trying to collect her thoughts and clear her head. And a smile spread slowly across her face as she realized the simple truth: there *were* no thoughts to collect, nothing in her mind to clear.

Saying those words had been so much simpler than she ever could have imagined. She felt suddenly free of him. And happy. It was like Scott's explanation of why people went to haunted houses, as if facing the monster had taken away all the pain.

She rose from her spot on the carpet and returned to the couch, still basking in a fresh new sense of personal empowerment. And she couldn't deny that she had Scott to thank.

Being with him had shown her that she didn't need someone fast and flashy to validate her, to make her feel good about herself. Being with him had shown her that she was pretty and sexy on her own. Or she *could* be, anyway. When she wasn't so busy being rude and indignant and cold. God, how she regretted the way she'd acted. What she wouldn't give to take it back.

But she had to push such fruitless thoughts from her mind. Scott was gone—she would never see him again. And even if she *should* chance to see him, she wouldn't know it; she didn't even know what he looked like without black and white paint on his face.

So it was silly to think about him, silly to regret things she couldn't change. No matter how many times thoughts of him kept sneaking back into her mind.

And yet she wondered, the next time she saw a man of his height and build, with thick, dark hair and chocolate brown eyes, wouldn't she wonder if that man was him? And wouldn't she wonder the next time? And the next time? How long before she would truly be able to erase him from her mind? If ever.

JULIE SPENT THE rest of the afternoon enjoying her novel, working to ignore the nagging feelings of regret that clawed inside her. Near six o'clock, as dusk faded to dark, she finished the last chapter and softly closed the book, setting it on the table next to her empty soup mug. She knew she'd better get up and turn on her porch light—the trick-or-treaters would be arriving soon.

She flipped the light switch and opened the big wooden door so she could see through the clear glass pane on the other side. Then she went to the kitchen where two trays of candy apples rested, already wrapped in cellophane with orange twist ties. Retrieving a sturdy wicker basket from the pantry, she loaded the apples inside.

Just then the doorbell rang, so she slid the basket's handle over her arm and went to answer. Just as she had suspected. A little ghost, along with a pint-sized Minnie Mouse, waited patiently on her porch.

"Trick or Treat," they both sang out before she could even reach the door.

"Ryan, is that you?" she asked the ghost. She only recognized the children from two doors down because their mother stood in the driveway watching.

"Yep, it's me," he said, holding his bag wide open.

"Well, that's a very scary costume. Yours is wonderful, too, Melissa."

"Mouse," she said from behind the Minnie mask.

"You make a very pretty mouse," Julie told her. Then she gently deposited a candy apple into each of their sacks, listening for their mumbled "thank yous" and sending them off with a wish of, "Happy Halloween."

The kids arrived in a constant stream after that, each cutely costumed and endearingly polite. Julie offered each one the same attention as the rest, admiring their outfits before bestowing their treat. She stepped outside in her socked feet a few times to carry on conversations with accompanying parents or grandparents, usually to have them tugged away by the children, anxious to move on to another house.

After an hour and a half, the foot traffic diminished. The streets no longer crawled with small animals and monsters and cartoon characters, and no more flashlights lit paths on the dark leaf-strewn sidewalks. It was again just a warm autumn night with blowing leaves and a cool, sweet breeze.

Stepping back outside, she peered up and down the street to make sure there were no more children on their way. After which she leaned her head back to gaze up at the stars in a freshly clear sky, the clouds from earlier all gone now.

And then she drew in her breath, unexpectedly remembering. They were the same stars she'd seen last night, out in the country, with Scott. The same bright moon shone down on the yard and through the trees that had lost most of their leaves.

She turned and went back into the house, pushing

the memory away. It brought back too many emotions—
and too many physical yearnings.

"Looks like its time for me to start on another book,"
she told herself aloud. Yes, that was what she'd do
tonight. Books were good for taking your mind off your
troubles, after all. Then tomorrow would be Monday
and she'd get up and go to the shop and things would be
normal again.

Normal again. Funny—she kept thinking things
were, but they still weren't. It was unsettling.

Glancing at the basket on the floor next to the door
revealed that only three candy apples remained. She
supposed it was a good thing trick-or-treating had ended
before she'd run out. In fact, it was good to know that
this entire pagan holiday had almost come to a close,
once and for all. *Maybe then. Maybe then things will be
normal.*

She returned to the kitchen to straighten up a little
and wash the few dishes she'd used for soup earlier. She'd
eaten nothing else today, though, and her stomach was
starting to growl. So maybe she would indulge in a candy
apple. Or maybe pop some popcorn. After finding some
in the pantry, she'd been just about to set the timer on
the microwave when the doorbell rang.

More trick-or-treaters. If there were more than three
she'd be sunk. But as she approached the glass door, she
saw that only one little fireman stood on her front stoop.

And then she caught her breath, but kept moving
toward the door. Even beneath that big red fire hat, she

recognized the child. He belonged to her new neighbor up the street. The gorgeous one with the dark hair and the tight jeans and the snuggly flannel shirts. The one who was hopefully single. The one whose existence she'd nearly forgotten about after all that had happened over the past twenty-four hours, but she knew Rhonda would kill her if she didn't look on this as an opportunity. And maybe it would get her mind off Scott.

She took a deep breath as she stepped up to the door and opened it. And she glanced around casually, but she didn't see a companion with the little boy, darn it.

"Trick or treat," he said in loud voice with a big smile.

Then she caught a glimpse of someone approaching slowly from the street—and was forced to suck in her breath again. It was the gorgeous dad. Looking just as gorgeous as ever. "Well," she said, lowering her gaze back to the little boy, "you're in luck. You're my last trick-or-treater of the night, so you get the rest of my candy apples."

The miniature fireman's eyes grew wide as they followed the path of the three apples from Julie's basket down into his bag. He smiled up at her, then turned to go—stopping only when his father, having reached the steps that led to her porch, gave the child a reproachful look. She found the sweet-but-trying-to-be-stern expression adorable on such a handsome man. And in response, the fireman turned back around and enunciated very clearly. "Thank you very much for the candy."

Julie smiled. What a sweet little guy. "You're very welcome. And you make a very handsome fireman."

"Thank you," he said proudly.

"Is that what you'd like to be when you grow up?" she asked.

"Nope," he said. "I want to be in the landscaping business like my dad."

"Oh," Julie said, using the convenient opening to glance toward the man who still stood in the shadows, "your dad's in the landscaping business."

The fireman nodded. "He says your yard needs a lot of work."

Which left her momentarily dumbfounded. "He does?"

"He says your crabapple tree needs to be pruned real bad and that your azaleas aren't gonna make it through the winter cuz you didn't do a fall mulching."

"Travis," his father finally reprimanded him.

"What, Dad?"

She could see the man's disconcerted smile in the dim lighting. "You're killing me here, son." He sounded a little embarrassed and...somehow familiar. But Julie didn't care about the condition of her yard. She only wanted to find a way to strike up a conversation with this handsome hunk of a man.

"Perhaps," she said, her eyes reaching timidly toward him, "we could strike up a deal. Free candy apples in trade for some landscaping advice?"

The hot dad stepped up closer, into the light, and

said, "Hi, I'm Scott," offering his hand. She took it and their eyes met. His were chocolate brown.

Julie gasped and grabbed at her throat with her free hand—then watched his eyes go wide.

"Witchiepoo?"

"Oh my God," she breathed.

"Oh my God is right," he mumbled.

Panic and leftover embarrassment had drawn her eyes away, but she made herself lift her gaze back to him. "You're my...my neighbor," she muttered as if he'd committed the worst crime imaginable.

"I guess I am."

"I didn't recognize you...without the bones...and the white stuff..." *On your beautiful face. On your beautiful, gorgeous, perfect face.*

"Well, I didn't recognize *you* without the...let's be honest here," he said, "without the dress."

Her eyes widened with a pang of distress. "That's all you remember about me? The dress?"

"No, of course not," he said. "But, well, face it, it was a great dress. Remember? All your sand was—"

"In all the right places," she finished for him—then tilted her head. "Still, that's all I was? Just an hourglass in a dress?"

"No," he said again. "You were...much more than that." He sighed, seeming exasperated with himself. And his voice softened. "You must know that."

She gently shook her head in disbelief.

"Well, you were. Things just got screwed up," he insisted. Then he nodded toward her feet. "How's your ankle?"

"Better," she said. "See? I'm walking again."

"I'm glad."

"Are you as bruised up as I am?" she asked.

"From head to toe," he replied.

She bit her lip, embarrassed. "Sorry I knocked you down so many times."

But he only let out a light laugh, his gaze upon her possibly the warmest thing she'd ever felt. "Don't worry, I'll live."

"Hey Dad, you know her?" Travis asked from below.

Scott looked down at his son. "Um, yeah, I do."

"You have a son," Julie acknowledged.

He nodded, his expression sheepish. "Guess I didn't I mention that."

"No, you didn't," she said. "But I'm beginning to think there's probably a *lot* you didn't mention."

"Like?"

"Well, you just seem so, so…" she motioned toward him with her hands, "…so different. So…settled. Even mature, although that might be stretching it."

He gave her a sexy grin beneath the dim glow of the porch light. "Even we skeletons have our mature sides."

Julie still felt overwhelmed by this new, unanticipated side of him—and she shook her head. "But why couldn't I see any of this in you last night?"

He tilted his head slightly, his chocolate eyes seeming to pour over her. "Well," he began slowly, "what did you tell me about masks?"

"What do you mean?"

"They're easy to hide behind. Easy to project another part of yourself from. Remember?"

She blinked when the meaning behind his words finally hit her. "So that wasn't really you last night?"

"Sure it was," he told her. "I mean, I'm a fun-loving guy and I certainly didn't lie to you about anything—but I'm also a responsible father, and I've run my own business since I was nineteen. A person can have more than one side to their personality. I just wish…" He stopped then, the darkness seeming to close around them as a cloud drifted across the moon. And Travis stood waiting below them as they peered helplessly into each other's eyes.

"What?" Julie asked. "What do you wish?"

"I wish things hadn't gotten so messed up between us," he said. "Right when they'd been going so good."

And her heart flooded with a glorious relief, her blood pumping like a teenager after the first kiss. "I know," she told him. "Me, too." Then she took a deep breath. "Only…what now?"

Scott held his hands out, seeming at a loss for words, something else she'd not seen in him before. "I'm not sure," he said. "Got any ideas?"

"Do you…want to come in for a while?" she ventured.

"What about your boyfriend?" he asked, peeking warily past her as if expecting to see someone lurking about.

Oh brother—she kept forgetting about that. But she swallowed back her shame about the silly fib and lifted her eyes to his. Honesty had been good to her with Scott, at least at some points in their brief relationship. And it had been scathingly good with Patrick earlier today. So she could find no reason not to be completely honest about this—now. And if she wanted to salvage anything with Scott, she didn't think she had a choice.

"What if I told you," she began cautiously, "that there never really *was* a boyfriend, but just an old ghost of one?"

A slow smile unfurl on Scott's gorgeous face. "Really?"

She nodded.

"Then I'd say I don't believe in ghosts," he replied.

And she smiled, too. "I don't, either. Not anymore."

Without warning, three small monsters jumped from behind the shrubs on the far side of her driveway, screaming, "*Boo!*" at the tops of their little lungs. Scott jerked to attention, while Julie nearly leaped out of her skin, and Travis gripped tightly onto his father's leg.

"Or on second thought," Scott said, "maybe I do."

"Quick. In here," she offered, holding the door wide open. "I'll protect you."

He hesitated for only a second before he scooped his son up beneath one arm, bag of candy and all, and stepped inside her front door.

Chapter Twelve

ONCE INSIDE, SCOTT set Travis gently on the floor and rose to face Julie. His brown eyes shone upon her as deep and consuming as any abyss, but there was still no disguising that it had suddenly become an awkward moment. "What do we do now?" he finally whispered.

She took a deep breath. "Eat popcorn?" she suggested.

"Yahoo!" Travis cried.

Which prompted Scott to reach down and pat his son on the top of his red plastic fireman's hat. "Yeah, that's just what he needs to start out a week of heavy candy eating."

"But can we, Dad? Can we?"

Scott glanced cautiously down at his son, then looked back at Julie, shrugging his approval. "This guy has me wrapped around his little finger," he admitted.

Which she couldn't deny was definitely working in her favor at the moment. "One great big bowl of buttered popcorn, coming up."

She headed to the kitchen to start the microwave. "Make yourselves comfortable by the fireplace," she yelled as she dug a large bowl from a cabinet beneath the counter.

Then, rising back up with the bowl in her grasp, she stopped and clutched it to her chest for a moment. God, she was nervous. Scott was here, suddenly back in her life. And she wanted him madly. But she had no idea how to proceed.

Stay cool. And be friendly. Yes, that was it. Who could go wrong with simply being friendly? It was a side of herself she displayed every day at the antique store, but one that Scott had, regrettably, not seen much of.

Then she glanced subtly around the corner into the living room, watching him with his son. The fact that he had a child stunned her. She'd never dated a man with a child before. But as she studied them privately, warm feelings drifted over her—who could resist an adorable kid like Travis? It was like having *The Courtship of Eddie's Father* right there in her living room. And now she wondered if she could be a part of their lives.

SCOTT LOWERED HIMSELF onto Julie's couch and ran his hands back through his hair. He couldn't believe this. Julie's couch. Julie's house. Julie, Julie, Julie, looking like the cutest thing he'd ever seen in that great big sweatshirt, her eyes shining up at him so nervously.

He watched his son climb up into an easy chair

across the room. "Be good for me, okay?" he whispered. He felt like a heel for not having told her he had a son—now he just hoped she liked kids.

"What's wrong, Dad?" Travis shot at him from across the room. "You're acting weird."

"Shhhhh," Scott said, letting his eyes go wide, a quieting finger at his lips. If Julie hadn't figured out for herself that he felt a little nervous, he'd prefer not to have Travis announce it.

He just hadn't been prepared to renew their rather volatile relationship so unexpectedly over candy apples. Not that he wasn't thrilled—he was practically overwhelmed. He just wished he'd known it was coming, that he'd had some warning. It had been easier last night in that damn skeleton suit.

And then he remembered what he'd been thinking about in front of the mirror when he'd finally gotten home last night. He'd wondered how it would have been between Julie and him if they'd met under normal circumstances. Well, he was about to find out.

JULIE TOOK A deep breath and leaned her head into the living room, no longer trying to hide. "What to drink?" she asked. "Soda, tea, milk, beer?"

"What do you say, buddy?" Scott asked Travis, who was perched in her easy chair, his little legs dangling off the edge, his hat tilted to the side.

"Beer please."

Scott cast his son a sideways glance. "You're burying me again here, pal." Then he looked up to Julie. "We'll both have sodas."

She couldn't help smiling. They were adorable together, father and son. And it was plain to see, even if Scott hadn't already admitted it, how crazy he was about the kid.

She served up Cokes and set the bowl of fluffy popcorn in the center of the coffee table. "So," she began, settling onto the couch next to Scott, but keeping a safe distance, "did you have a good time Trick or Treating tonight, Travis?"

He nodded as he took a long sip of soda through the curly-cue straw she'd found in a kitchen drawer. "But you're the only person who invited us in for extra stuff."

She bit her lip as a thin heat of embarrassment climbed her face, then glanced at Scott, who returned her look with an amused grin. "So do you invite *all* your Trick or Treaters inside?" he asked.

She shook her head flirtatiously, then whispered, "Only the ones with the good-looking dads."

"Oh," he said with a grin, "I pass the test then."

"There never *was* any test," she promised him. "That's the truth. I didn't care what you looked like."

His warm eyes seemed to dig beneath the surface as he gazed at her then—and she could have sworn the room had grown smaller, containing only the two of them, just as the porch had moments ago. In her mind she traveled back to the previous night, to how close they'd been, how much they'd touched. She remembered his tongue in the valley between her breasts. She could barely breathe.

"How about a ghost story?" she said to break the tension.

Scott laughed, while Travis cheered the idea. "Yeah, a ghost story," he said.

"Go ahead," she motioned to Scott.

"Me?" he asked with raised eyebrows.

"Sure," she said. "You're a dad. You should be good at this."

"I usually work with a script. Dr. Seuss, Walt Disney, those guys."

She smiled. "Well, here's your chance to show what you've learned."

"What I've learned," he mused. "Okay, I'll give it a try."

Julie leaned back on her end of the couch and pulled her knees up to her chest while Travis leaned forward on his chair to listen attentively.

"It was a dark and scary night," Scott began, his eyes on Travis. "And Daryl Dukes was on the loose."

"Who's Daryl Dukes?" Travis asked his dad.

"Crazy guy," Scott said. "Walks around in the dark with a scary flashlight looking for innocent people to terrorize."

Travis's eyes grew wide. "Does he find any?"

Scott hesitated. "He finds a very pretty woman and a very nice man," he replied, casting a quick look at Julie.

"They're sitting together on a school bus."

"On a school bus?" Travis asked, clearly perplexed. "School buses are for kids."

"Well, they were taking a walk out in the country when it began to rain," Scott explained. "They saw an old abandoned bus, so they climbed on board to keep dry."

"Okay. What happened next?"

"Well, the man and the woman were…getting to know each other," Scott said. Travis nodded as if he knew exactly what that meant. "When out of the darkness appeared Daryl Dukes with his crazy flashlight!"

Travis leaned back in his seat, his eyes suddenly fraught with terror.

"He climbed up on the bus and he said, 'Who the heck are you?' The very nice man explained that he and the woman had been taking a walk and gotten on the bus when it started to rain. *And just when they thought Daryl was going to kill them*," Scott said, his voice rising to a dramatic crescendo, "he didn't."

"He didn't?" Travis repeated, obviously surprised, his little brow furrowing. "What did he do then?"

"He gave them a ride back to town."

Travis looked forlorn. And sleepy. "Huh?"

"See, Trav, sometimes people aren't exactly what they seem. Turns out Daryl Dukes was actually a pretty nice guy, despite what the pretty woman and the nice man assumed. He wasn't so crazy after all."

Julie's heart warmed as she took in the meaning behind Scott's story. "And maybe you aren't so rude and bossy, after all," she whispered beneath her breath.

"And maybe you're not so mean," Scott replied.

A jolt of powerful emotion gripped her tightly then—that same crazy, whirlwind feeling that had hit her last night. She had thought it love at the time. Could it be?

Scott pulled his gaze from her only to glance at his son. "Little guy's conking out on us," he said.

She looked to Travis slumped in his chair, his fireman's hat falling down over his eyes, and couldn't resist a smile at his sweet innocence.

"Mind if I move him to the couch?" Scott asked.

She shook her head and stood. Then watched as Scott gently scooped the boy into his arms and lay him on the couch, tucking a throw pillow beneath his head. He softly removed the red hat and laid it on the coffee table next to the popcorn bowl.

Julie settled on the thick rug in front of the fireplace, and when Scott joined her, she fought to push down the adolescent rush of nerves that returned with his sudden nearness.

"Seems like a great kid," she said.

"Yeah, Trav is the best."

"Why didn't you tell me about him?" she asked with an inquisitive smile.

He swallowed and glanced down—then looked back at her. "Let me explain something," he said. "I'm crazy about Travis. He's the number one thing in my life.

But…"

"But?"

He cast another sheepish grin. "Six-year-old boys are not exactly chick magnets."

She laughed softly. "So I'm a chick now."

"No. You were. I mean, when I first saw you."

"What changed?"

"I don't know." He shook his head. "Maybe I somehow saw a nice person beneath all that pretend stuff, beneath all that anger. Still, I just didn't see a reason to mention him. It's the kind of complicated stuff I don't feel comfortable laying on just anybody."

She shrugged, asking, "Have I passed the 'just anybody' mark yet?"

He offered a light smile in reply.

"So lay it on me," she said.

Then watched as he took a deep breath. "I told you it was a bad divorce."

She nodded.

"Well, the main thing that was bad about it was that my ex-wife put me through hell fighting over custody of Travis. She kept threatening to move him away from me, to make it hard for me to see him. And then, in the end, after she'd nearly driven me crazy with all the threats and fighting, she suddenly just gave it up. She didn't want him anymore."

"She gave up custody?" Julie asked, eyebrows shooting upward.

Next to her, Scott let out a sad sigh. "Now she hardly

even visits the kid. Birthdays and Christmas. Maybe an occasional weekend now and then." He lifted his gaze to her, adding, "It's hard as hell to explain to a little boy why his mommy doesn't come to see him."

Julie was aghast. "I can't believe any woman could do that to a child."

"I couldn't either," Scott said, "before I saw it, and lived it."

"It must be hard, just the two of you," she offered.

But he only shrugged. "Not really. He's a good kid. And my mom helps out a lot; she lives just a few minutes from here."

"That's good. I think every child should have both a man and a woman in his life if possible."

He smiled thoughtfully in response. "Yeah, I can tell he misses that sometimes. And I think he was pretty flattered with all those candy apples. And then inviting us in and giving us popcorn. You're going to be pretty popular with him."

"Well, he's already pretty popular with me," she confessed. "He's adorable."

"Yeah, especially when he's making me look bad," Scott grumbled playfully. "He's *really* adorable then."

They both laughed softly, and Julie asked, "So…is my yard really in that bad of shape?"

He hesitated. "Well, I didn't exactly plan for Mr. Big Mouth over there to go telling you about it, but…yeah, it could use some work."

"I'm not too outdoorsy," she admitted. "Inside, I'm a

whiz. I can decorate and design. I can find just the right place for everything in a room. But outdoors, I'm all thumbs. And not green ones."

"I might be able to help you out."

"Yeah?"

"I can send some guys over here this week to do some pruning and mulching. And, by the way, you've got a bad thatch problem brewing, too. But that can wait until next summer."

She gave her head a playful tilt. "And do I get these services for free or what?"

"Mmm, almost free," he said.

She widened her eyes, met his gaze head on. "Okay, name your price."

"I want you to tell me," he began softly, "about this ghost of a boyfriend."

She hadn't seen that coming and answered with a sigh. But she knew she owed him yet more honesty—and she only hoped she could explain without totally embarrassing herself.

"Four months ago," she began, "Patrick broke up with me to move in with a girl he had been cheating on me with for a year."

"Oh," he said, obviously taken aback. "I'm sorry." Then he swallowed. "So maybe we have more in common than I realized." His words reminded her that he, too, knew the pain of an unfaithful companion.

"Patrick is…a player," Julie tried to explain. "He's good-looking, lots of fun, a big spender. He's got a voice as smooth as silk and can literally charm the pants off any woman he meets."

Scott's brow knit slightly. "Even with my limited knowledge of you, this guy doesn't sound to me like someone you would be with."

"I know," she said. "I'm just now figuring that out, too. He never made me feel good about myself. He said he loved me without having the faintest idea what that meant. And his entire life revolves around sex. With absolutely anyone who will have him."

He gave his head a doubtful tilt. "And you're still crazy about this loser?"

"No," she said softly, realizing that it really was true now. "It took me a while to get over him—because for a while, in the beginning, he made me happy and I guess I just kept wanting more of that, thinking I could somehow get back to how things once were. But he called me today and said he wanted me back—and I told him I'd moved on."

He raised his eyebrows. "Yeah?"

"Yeah. And I really meant it. I *have* moved on. In here," she said, pointing to her heart. "And I sort of...owe it all to you."

"Whoa," he said, surprised. "Really?"

"Look, I don't want to sound super corny here or anything, but last night," she said, her voice softening, "you changed the way I see myself. You made me feel good about not only about how I looked but also who I was underneath that. And you made me realize that it was all right to have fun."

He lowered his chin. "I didn't realize you'd *had* any fun last night."

"Despite myself," she said, peering over at him, "I did. With you."

"I had fun with you, too," he said. "And even after the way things ended…well, I haven't been able to get you off my mind."

Her heart swelled. "Even after I was so mean to you?"

"Even after. Did you cast a spell on me, Witchie-poo?" he asked sweetly, making her smile. "I wished I hadn't left you at your friend's apartment last night. I wished I'd taken you home with me whether you liked it or not. I was sure I'd never see you again."

"Me, too."

"Julie," he whispered, "you made me start thinking."

"About what?"

He took a deep breath. "After my marriage ended, I never wanted to trust someone again. I took my vows seriously and having my marriage fail was the worst thing that's ever happened to me. But after being with you last night, I started thinking…about caring for a woman. About commitment. And I realized something. It's not something you choose, a decision you make. It's something that either happens or it doesn't—it's there or it's not." He reached over and took one of her hands in his. "And with you, well, I think it might be there."

Julie couldn't believe her ears. Was this the man she'd known last night? He was right—the luxury of a hidden face could change everything. "Really?" she breathed.

"I can't make promises to you," Scott said softly. "I wouldn't want to make one that I couldn't keep. And we just met, after all. But if you can be patient with me, I might be able to make one…sometime."

She titled her head, gazed into his eyes. "I can be patient."

"That easily?" he asked, his expression registering surprise. "Are you sure?"

"That easily," she replied. "See, I did some thinking, too. And I realized that when we were in that bus…"

"Getting to know each other," he volunteered with a grin.

"Yes," she said with a quick smile of her own—but then let it fade to something a little more serious. "I realized that I wanted you with or without promises. That I was crazy enough about you to risk it. And I still am."

"You're crazy about me?" he asked with raised eyebrows.

"That surprises you?"

"Um, yeah. I mean, I thought you'd started liking me some, but…"

"Remember," she told him, her voice dropping to a soft whisper, "how things were in the bus."

"How close we were," he whispered back.

"How you touched me."

"Yes."

"Kissed me."

"I wanted you so much," he said, his voice growing deeper.

"And *I* wanted *you*," she breathed.

"I know I just told you I couldn't make promises, Julie, but I'd be lying if I said I wasn't crazy about you, too."

She sighed, suddenly filled with more hope than she'd thought she'd ever feel again. Her heart quaked in her chest and her lips trembled with longing. "Oh Scott," she whispered, the desire cascading through her voice.

Lifting his hand to her cheek, he pushed her hair back from her face as he leaned in to gently brush his lips across hers.

She hissed at the tease of pleasure—and when his mouth returned, it met hers fully this time and she let herself sink into him, becoming intoxicated with the kiss she'd thought she'd never have more of.

His arms came slowly around her to lay her gently back on the rug as he kissed her more voraciously now. And when he rolled on top of her, their legs intertwining—first loosely, then locking together more tightly—she experienced the thick rise of pleasure at the crux of her thighs.

His sexy mouth was on her face, in her hair, dancing across the tender skin of her neck. His hands dug beneath the long sweatshirt she wore, bunching the material at her midriff as he kneaded her bare waist with his strong hands.

She sighed as his hand rose, gently gliding across her skin until it slid over the cup of her bra—and she drew in her breath at the touch, so private and so perfect. He caressed her breast, at first softly, then more deeply, the sensation driving her wild. And she heard herself panting as her fingers clawed through his hair, clutching at his head and his shoulders, whatever parts of him she could touch and pull closer.

Then he stopped and raised his head, glancing toward Travis, sleeping soundly on the sofa.

"Let's go outside," he whispered hotly down to her.

"Outside?"

"Where Travis won't hear, where we can be alone."

"Like last night," she said, a smile playing about her lips.

His gazed at her sexily. "Like last night."

Scott's eyes on her were wild, inciting a rush inside her that she couldn't control. He hopped to his feet and held his hands down to her, and she rose just as quickly, with his help, careful not to twist her ankle again, but in a hurry to be alone with him. Nothing else in the world seemed more important.

"Will Travis be okay in here?" she asked.

Scott nodded. "Kid sleeps like a log."

Taking her hand, he led her out the front door and the cool evening air enveloped her with memories of the previous night, fueling her passion. "Where will we go?" she whispered.

"The backyard?" he suggested.

"Yes."

When he stopped and scooped her into his arms again, she pressed against him, kissing his neck, clutching at his shoulders, savoring the feeling of being held by him once more.

Her backyard was a circus of moonlit red and golden leaves. The huge trees behind her house, as well as the woods beyond, created a carpet of brilliant fall colors. When he finally set her on her feet beneath the cover of trees, their gazes met, fiery and hot, as he gently leaned her back against the trunk of a large maple. "I want this so much," he murmured.

His hands ran solidly over her breasts before dropping to her hips—then he pressed his body into hers, grinding against her until she wanted to explode.

A soft moan escaped her lips just before more of his kisses filled her senses, somehow both wild and gentle at the same time. "I want to see you," he whispered. "I want to see what I missed out on in that school bus."

Julie pushed him back slightly. She wanted him to see her, too. And when his eyes were planted firmly upon her, she reached down to the edges of the big sweatshirt and lifted it off over her head.

She glanced down at the gentle swell of her breasts rising from her simple white lace bra, then returned her gaze to Scott. His eyes were wild with want. And his voice was raspy, less than a whisper. "Please take it off for me."

She trembled as she reached behind her back and unhooked the bra, letting it linger there, loosened around her, the straps resting on the edges of her shoulders. She closed her eyes, drinking in the incredible pleasure of the moment. Then she pulled the bra away, letting it drop to the ground below.

Scott moaned at the sight, his eyes still locked upon her, seemingly mesmerized. But as he took a step forward, she put up a hand to silently halt him.

"I want you to just look at me for a little while," she told him in a rough whisper, surprised yet scintillated by her own words. "Just look at me." Then she leaned back against the tree trunk, lifting her arms above her head to claw at the heavy bark. She pressed her back against the tree, stretching like a cat as he watched her sensual movements.

Last night, at the party, men's eyes had felt rude and invasive, but Scott's eyes, now, were more welcome on her than anything she could imagine. She could feel his gaze, pouring over her, almost touching her somehow, and she was filled with amazement at how much pleasure it gave her.

Her own eyes brimming with desire, she finally issued him a silent command—and he moved toward her then, too brusquely to be stopped even if she'd wanted to. His hands raked over her behind, then moved quickly around to her bare breasts, so white beneath the moonlight, their rosy tips dark and inviting. Then he sank his mouth there, quickly sending Julie into spasms of bliss.

"Yes," she whispered to him as he licked and sucked at her. "Oh yes."

When she pushed him away from her once again, his mouth was reluctant to leave—but she needed to get to his body now, needed to unbutton his shirt, which she did almost frantically, revealing the strong, hard chest beneath.

She first ran her hands over the taut muscles, then repeated the motion with only the tips of her fingernails, making him moan as she gently raked through the soft, dark hair that dusted his chest.

Leaning inward, she sprinkled soft kisses there, afterward taking one nipple between her lips. It quickly beaded beneath her tongue and he moaned. She pulled back to lick gentle circles around it.

"You're making me crazy," he breathed. "I want you so much."

"I want you to do *everything* to me," she replied.

With that, he began to work at the button of her blue jeans, releasing it quickly. He yanked down the zipper, then shoved the jeans toward the ground. Kneeling to help her step out of them, he afterward leaned in to kiss the front of her silk panties.

"Oh," she breathed. Her lips trembled at the incredible sensations swirling through her and she was forced to lean back against the tree for support.

She didn't protest when Scott, still on his knees, reached up to peel those panties down. She bit her lip and let herself drown anew in the pleasure of his gaze—

then closed her eyes to drink in more kisses, this time coming on the soft tuft of hair that was usually hidden.

She released a tender moan. Then felt his tongue. Opening her. Slicing into her with a thick, racing pleasure. Making her spread her legs for him.

Julie clawed at the trunk above her head, finally spreading her arms to grab onto the branches at either side. She gripped at them tightly, the bark rough on her palms, but hardly noticeable compared to the beautiful vibrations below.

When Scott finally leaned back to look up at her, he licked his lips and whispered, "You are so beautiful."

She couldn't speak, though—could only open her mouth and let a soft moan of desire leak free.

"I want to be inside you," he said, the words wafting over her like sweet ecstasy.

"I want that, too," she managed now. "I want it more than anything. And I want it now."

Scott rose to his feet and hurriedly pushed his blue jeans to the ground, then his briefs. He looked incredible. So strong and hard. So ready to love her.

"Help me," he said.

"What?" she murmured, her eyes rising to his face.

And in response, he held out a packaged condom he'd retrieved from his jeans.

She bit her lip, raised her gaze to his eyes. "You were expecting this when you set out Trick or Treating?"

"You never know," he said with a wink. "You might not have come through with the candy."

"Then this would be the trick," she said.

He tilted his head sideways, reconsidering. "On second thought, I think this is definitely an extra treat. Travis got his. This is mine."

Taking the packet from his fingers, she ripped into it and pulled out the flat, rolled condom, her heartbeat increasing at the thought of what she was about to do.

Scott took a step toward her and she trembled. "Put it on me," he said.

She flashed him a wild look laced with uncertainty.

"Don't be afraid," he told her. "I want you to touch me."

Dropping slowly to her knees, letting them crunch in the colored leaves, she shivered at how close she was to him, to that part of him. Then, with trembling fingers, she reached out to gently sheathe him. He sighed at her feathery touches, then sank to his knees as well, facing her, ready, their eyes meeting with the heat of anticipation.

He gently pushed at the inside of her thighs with both hands, spreading her legs and sending a hot thrill racing up her center. She had never been more ready for anything in her life.

Then he firmly grabbed her behind and softly thrust himself into her. She felt herself open to him and moaned as he entered.

She soon lay on her back, leaves crushing beneath her as she moved with his fullness. His kisses covered her face and she yearned for more.

Then he rolled over onto his back, pulling her along with him, so that she lay on top. His thrusts filled her, again and again, and she moved in a rhythm that grew hotter until she was sitting upright, straddling him, riding him in tight, churning circles.

"I want to make you feel good," he whispered up to her.

Had anyone ever said that to her before? She didn't think so. And Scott meant it, she knew. She could feel it in the warm, sensual way he moved beneath her. In the way he heated up, but then slowed down, taking his time. For her. All for her.

A deep ecstasy began building inside her, like a wall she was climbing, or a treasure she grew nearer and nearer to finding. She leaned her head back and imagined she was drowning in the stars. The stars and Scott. They were the only things that existed in that moment. The only things that mattered.

And then came the sweet release. The unbelievable burst of pleasure. The overwhelming joy that coursed through her veins and vibrated through her skin from head to toe. All-consuming, the spasms that rocked her were almost violent in their strength, yet filled her with the deepest satiation she'd ever known.

As her waves subsided, they began for Scott. He moaned beneath her, thrusting up into her harder, stronger, filling her even more. Then he lay there, still, quiet, his eyes closed in what seemed a private moment of ecstasy, something she couldn't penetrate and didn't want to. She'd wanted to make him feel good, too. And she knew he was basking in the pleasure she'd given him.

When he opened his eyes to look up at her, his gaze was no longer wild, but warmer, sweeter again. Those deep chocolate eyes melted her.

"I…" she faltered, then broke into a wide smile.

"What is it, honey?" he whispered.

She shook her head slightly, then told him. "That never happened before."

"What never happened?" he asked sweetly.

"I…um, never knew it could feel like that."

He tilted his head below her in the leaves, gazing up inquisitively. "Julie," he whispered, "are you saying that you've never come with a man before?"

She bit her lip, considering. "I don't think anyone's ever really cared if I felt good before. Until now. You."

"Oh baby," he said, pulling her down into a hug, "I can't believe any man wouldn't want to make you feel good."

"I want to make you feel good, too," she whispered into his chest.

And a wicked smile took shape on his face. "No problem there."

Then they both heard the muffled voice coming from within the house. "Dad?"

Julie raised her head and looked down at Scott with alarm. "I'm coming, Trav," he leaned around her to yell through the darkness. "I'll be there in a minute."

"Where are you, Dad?"

"Just stay where you are, son. I'll be right in." Then he looked up at Julie above him. "Um, I'm afraid this is the part where he isn't exactly a chick magnet."

She shook her head. "I don't mind."

"Then *you*," he said, rolling out from under her to grab for his boxer briefs, "are one understanding woman."

"All chicks aren't alike, you know." She reached for her panties and worked to pull them on.

"So you like my kid," he said, hurrying to yank up his blue jeans, "even though he just interrupted a near-perfect sexual encounter."

"Well, at least he let us finish."

Scott threw on his shirt and offered an exaggerated shiver, as if perishing the thought had Travis yelled out a few moments before.

"Go on in," she said, still sitting in the leaves, working to disentangle her inside-out sweatshirt. "I'll be there in a second."

"Sure you're all right out here? I mean, I don't feel like I got to say all the things I wanted to, like how gorgeous you are and how wonderful that was."

She smiled up at him.

"Dad?"

"Go ahead," she prodded. "I'm deliriously happy. I promise."

Julie listened as Scott jogged back around the house through the crunching leaves. Then she sat there, absorbing the beauty of the moment. The silence. The stars. The moon. The overwhelming contentment flowing through every limb of her body. She wanted to squeeze every ounce of joy from it she could.

She rose and found the rest of her clothing, the realization hitting her that she'd just made love in her backyard on a clearly moonlit night. But just as Scott had made her understand the evening before, being a little naughty wasn't so horrible when you did it with the right person.

She stepped back into her jeans and slid the big sweatshirt on over her head, then walked back around the house in her still sock-covered feet.

"Everything okay in here?" she asked as she stepped inside the door.

Scott sat on the couch with Travis perched in his lap. "Yeah," Scott said. "Trav was just a little surprised when he woke up and I wasn't here. Weren't you, buddy?"

"I wasn't scared or anything," he told Julie.

"No, of course not," she said.

"Just a little worried, right?" Scott asked.

Travis nodded.

"So I explained to him that you and I had just gone out for a walk," Scott continued, offering a quick wink in her direction. "And now he wants to go for a walk, too."

"You can come with us," Travis offered to her.

"Really?" Julie asked. "I'd like that very much."

Scott shook his head. "Maybe tomorrow, buddy. It's a school night and I've kept you out pretty late already."

"Tomorrow after school?" Travis suggested in Julie's

direction. Scott looked up, too, his expression almost as eager.

"Tomorrow it is," she replied.

"And you can watch me ride my bike if you want."

"That sounds like fun."

"And you can even watch me toss ball with Dad, too."

She smiled again.

"Now, Trav," Scott said, "Julie might not want to spend *all* her time watching you do things."

"Oh, there's nothing I'd love more," Julie corrected him. "I mean, the kid's a regular chick magnet."

Scott smiled. Then he rose from the couch and plunked Travis' red hat down on his head. "Let's go home and examine all this candy," he said to his son. "And after your bath, maybe you can have one of Julie's Caramel apples."

Then Scott lifted his eyes to Julie as he reached out for her hand. "Hey," he whispered. "Thank you." He closed his warm brown eyes as he leaned in to drop a soft kiss on her cheek. "You're enough to make me believe in happy endings again."

Epilogue

————— ⌁ —————

"WELL," RHONDA'S VOICE boomed through the phone, "I guess you're happy Halloween's finally over."

"Why, whatever do you mean?" Julie responded in her Scarlett O'Hara voice. "I think it's a perfectly charmin' little holiday."

"Oh?" Rhonda inquired dryly. "Okay. What am I missing? What's going on here?"

"No time to talk," Julie teased. "I've gotta run. I have a date with two great guys."

Rhonda stayed silent a moment. "You *are* kidding. I know you are. Because I'm the kinky one here and even I'm not *that* kinky."

"No," Julie said. "I'm not kidding at all. Now, I've gotta go. They're going to be waiting."

"Ohhhhhhhh," Rhonda said, the lightbulb apparently finally clicking on. "I get it. It's the neighbor. The neighbor and the kid. Your ship came in. Your wishes came true. All that stuff. Is that it, Jules? Please tell me it is, and then please plan lunch with me tomorrow so you can tell me everything."

"Okay. Yes, it's the neighbor and his son. And it's going to take much longer than lunch. Possibly a ten-course dinner would provide enough time."

"I realize it's good news," Rhonda said, re-effecting her dry tone. "But how much can there be to tell about a date made over the distribution of candy apples?"

"I'll give you a hint. My neighbor looks excellent in bones."

It took a moment for Rhonda to figure out what Julie was saying—and then it finally hit her. "What? No!"

"Yes."

"No! No! No!"

"Scott's here, I've gotta run. We're going rollerskating."

"Jules, don't you dare hang up this phone before—"

"Gotta go, Rhonda. Bye."

Julie hung up, then grabbed a jacket and headed out the door. She found Travis's face pressed up against the back seat window of Scott's car, his mouth in the shape of an "o". As Scott glanced back at his son as she approached, she heard his muffled words through the car's closed windows. "You're killing me again, Trav."

She climbed in the car knowing that nothing could pull her away from this guy. He hadn't offered her promises, but he'd offered her all that he could. His passion. His tenderness. His sweetness. A place in his life, *their* lives. And when she looked into his eyes, she saw all the promise she needed.

"Hi there," he said, smiling.

"Hi," she replied.

"So, are you ready for this?"

Was she ready? More than he could know. She wasn't afraid anymore. Of the man, or his love. Or the love she felt for him. She had the feeling that this was the beginning of something good, the beginning of something real, and the beginning of something that might just last forever.

Look for more classic Toni Blake reissues, including:

The Cinderella Scheme
The Guy Next Door

And don't miss any of these contemporary romance titles
from Toni Blake:

The Coral Cove Series:
All I Want Is You
Love Me If You Dare
Take Me All The Way

The Destiny Series:
One Reckless Summer
Sugar Creek
Whisper Falls
Holly Lane
Willow Springs
Half Moon Hill

Other Titles:
Wildest Dreams
The Red Diary
Letters to a Secret Lover
Tempt Me Tonight
Swept Away

About the Author

Toni Blake's love of writing began when she won an essay contest in the fifth grade. Soon after, she penned her first novel, nineteen notebook pages long. Since then, Toni has become a RITA™-nominated author of more than twenty contemporary romance novels, her books have received the National Readers Choice Award and Bookseller's Best Award, and her work has been excerpted in *Cosmo*. Toni lives in the Midwest and enjoys traveling, crafts, and spending time outdoors. Learn more about Toni and her books at www.toniblake.com, or sign up for her newsletter and follow her on Facebook to get all the latest news and have a chance to win signed books and other prizes.